CONCERTO

SKYE WARREN

CHAPTER ONE

"When I wished to sing of love, it turned to sorrow. And when I wished to sing of sorrow, it turned to love." – Franz Schubert

SAMANTHA

T HE THEATER RISES above the city, an old-world counterpoint to a modern melody. Rounded cobblestones curve the thin cardboard of my ballet flats. Water rushes with quiet urgency from a fountain.

"Should we go in?" Josh says, his tone laconic. "Or should we just stare at it more?"

I give him a pointed look. "Impatient, much?"

Okay, so I might be a little nervous. And I might have stood here, taking deep breaths, fortifying myself, for more than five minutes. This is my first major tour, which is enough to make any musician nervous. Even more than that, it's my first performance after turning eighteen.

No one can call me a child prodigy anymore.

I'm no longer a child.

I lift my chin and step up to the heavy front

doors. There must be more practical entrances around the sides, but I don't want to go skulking around the building. The email inviting me to practice had been terse. *You may arrive at 9 a.m. Mrs. Tabakov will meet you.*

Josh knocks on the carved wooden doors, the sound reverberating in a way that makes me feel like we're waking some long-slumbering dragon. A pause, long enough to make me glance at Josh.

"Last chance to turn back."

"No way," I say, even though my heart thumps in warning.

The door opens. I'm expecting Mrs. Tabakov to be a woman with grey hair and a stern mouth, someone who's managed generations of performers and rules backstage with an iron fist. Instead the most beautiful woman I've ever seen stands there in a glittering gold gown and bare feet, golden curls tumbling around her shoulders.

"Call me Candy. And you must be Samantha Brooks," she says with a smile. "So lovely to meet you."

Shyness makes my tongue heavy. "Are you Mrs. Tabakov?"

"That's me. I'm the owner of the Grand."

"Oh wow." She's so young to own such a historic building, but I know better than most how age has nothing to do with your achievements. "It's such an honor to be able to play here."

She looks at Josh in a frank, assessing way. "Is this your lover?"

I cough in surprise, my cheeks turning pink. "No, no, definitely not."

"You had to say no three times?" Josh asks, extending his hand. "Joshua North. Personal security."

"He's like family to me," I say, apologetic.

"That didn't stop you with Liam," he says under his breath, and I have to force myself to not kick him in the shin. Even though…he's not wrong.

Liam North got custody of me when I was twelve. His guardianship ended two weeks ago, when I turned eighteen and left his home. I'm not empty-handed. I have the incredible Stradivarius violin he gave me for my birthday on one hand. And I have his brother, Joshua North, who's going to be my bodyguard after a suspicious accident at home.

It's impossible for me to define my relationship with Liam. Parental? Romantic? It was neither of those things—and both of them. We forged our own bond, as unique as it was temporary.

I have to find my own path now—one that begins here, at the Grand.

A man appears behind Candy, his expression severe. From the silver threading his temples, it's clear he's older than her. The hand he curves around her waist leaves no doubt as to his claim. "Ivan Tabakov," he says, a layer of steel beneath his words as he stares down Josh. "I will arrange a meeting between you and our head of security. In the meantime, I can show you the important features."

"Perfect," Candy says, smiling up at him. "That way I can have some girl time with Samantha. It's not every day I get to meet a world-famous violinist."

Josh raises an eyebrow at me before following Ivan outside.

I'm relieved, though I don't say that as I follow Candy into the theater. Josh has been in turns taunting and autocratic, like an annoying older brother. If we were both years younger, he would probably steal my dolls and I would paint glitter on his Legos. Instead we've resorted to exchanging insults over the room service cart while we try to stay out of sight of paparazzi.

The paparazzi don't care about me. I'm not an

interesting figure except in the world of classical music, but the headliner of the tour is a different story. Celebrity tenor Harry March loves the red carpet almost more than he loves music. He's been seen with pop stars and actresses and heiresses.

We step into an open foyer with red carpet and two wide staircases curving to a balcony. The wall between them extends all the way to the ceiling, forty feet high. There's a dark painting of a forest, the branches almost reaching out from the wall.

"That's incredible," I breathe. "Are there—" It felt like there were creatures lurking between the trees. I had the impression of doe-tipped siren eyes, like otherworldly wood nymphs. When I tried to focus on one particular creature, it would disappear into swirls of painted leaves.

"I know. It's painted by Harper St. Claire. Do you know her?"

"Only on Instagram. I didn't realize she had an installation here."

"There's an art gallery with another one of her works, as well as pieces by local artists. I'll show you another time. I'm grateful that the Tanglewood art community has embraced this place, considering it used to be a strip club."

My cheeks turn hot. "I thought that was a rumor."

Candy runs a hand over the balcony, almost caressing, the way you might show affection for a person. "The lady has a sordid past. Are you going to hold it against her?"

She isn't speaking of a lady, she's talking about the Grand. I think of the Stradivarius I hold, the Lady Tennant. It was given that name because of its initial owner, but most violins are considered feminine. Most buildings, too. "Of course not," I say. "She isn't responsible for what people do inside her, is she?"

Only when the words come out of my mouth do I realize the filthy connotation. Or maybe it's the light of humor in Candy's blue eyes that makes the words dirty. It isn't a mocking amusement, though. It's as if we're sharing a joke, the three of us—Candy, me, and the building herself.

"I imagine you're eager to see the stage and begin practice." She leads me behind the box office, where velvet stairs take us up. Rows of seats form a scalloped shadow. Then we crest the gallery, revealing the stage. Breath rushes from my lungs. A wide arc of hardwood—not gleaming and smooth, as from a new stack of wood. This stage is weathered, as if from a thousand feet, a hundred songs. A million hopes and dreams.

At least some of those dreams belonged to strippers.

Like the one beside me. I don't think I'm mistaken about the role she used to play.

Candy coughs delicately. "Some musicians don't want to play the Grand."

There's something erotic in the curls of gilding on the balconies, a sense of unveiling in the heavy falls of red curtains. Something of the strip club remains—its spirit, more than form. "It will be an honor," I tell her. "And besides. We have Harry March as the headliner. He's not exactly a choir boy."

"Thank God for that," she says fervently, and I laugh.

"I'm a little nervous about it actually."

"His reputation." She winks at me. "I bet he'll show you a good time."

"That's what I'm nervous about."

It's her turn to laugh.

I wander down the aisle, trailing my fingers over hard-backed seats and golden wood arms. A downward slope speeds my step until I near the orchestra pit. Only a short black wall separates the front row from the conductor. Empty chairs hold the place for violins and cellos and basses. For clarinets and French horns. Deep beneath the stage there's a grand piano and a harp.

I climb the steps to the stairs, holding my breath. This is where I'll play my first note as an adult musician. This is where I'll launch my music career, free of the fear and the tenuous safety of my childhood. It's bittersweet to know that Liam North won't see me play.

"You have the place to yourself," Candy says from the first row, her voice carrying in the strong acoustics. "Mr. March doesn't arrive for a week, and the other performers a week after that."

From this position I can't see the back row or the balcony. It's a blur of shadowy seats. Someone could be sitting there, and I wouldn't know. A shiver runs down my spine. "We'll be practicing for two months. Don't you have other shows?"

"We're selective about what we present." She smiles, a little self-deprecating. "The truth is we don't need the money. The Grand is my passion."

The tour will take us to some of the largest venues in the world, the concert hall Heifetz favored and the place Paganini once stood. I don't know exactly why the Grand was chosen to debut the tour. It was probably something cold and calculating, like favorable percentage in the contracts. Maybe even a performer's bonus for Harry March. Whatever the reason, I'm glad it happened that way.

"What if you hadn't liked me when I showed up here?"

She gives me an impish smile. "What makes you think I like you?"

I look around. "Would I be standing here if you didn't?"

"Probably not. Ivan is my husband, but he's also my personal security."

I remember his cold eyes. He wouldn't be someone I'd want as my enemy. I can't imagine him softening, except that someone like Candy could probably melt an iceberg. She's got this sensual way of walking and talking and basically breathing.

"There are chairs behind the stage. If you'd like something in particular—"

"I'll stand for today. It's the way I'll perform, after all."

"Then I'll leave you to it," she says with a small curtsey that seems both graceful and majestic. Then it's just me standing on a massive stage in front of thousands of empty seats.

I set down the case for my violin and sit down cross-legged, taking it out with slow care and applying rosin to the bow. There is a ritual to playing in front of other people. There are ghosts in the seats this afternoon. They watch me close my eyes and position my violin.

They hold their collective breath as I rest the bow to the strings. I have to push aside my grief over Liam North. My uncertainty over a future spent alone. A tour that can change the course of my life. A moving performance can inspire a scientist or sway a politician to kindness. The potential and the risk fade away. A sweet note enters the air, and I play.

LIAM

THERE'S A SOUND that fills my nightmares—the smack of fist against flesh. Except this isn't a dream. The splinter of bone as it gives way. The man at my feet groans. He is relatively unharmed, compared to how he'll end the evening. "You could make this easier," I say in fluent Russian. "Tell me where he is."

He spits blood at me, which I don't bother to wipe from my face. I'm covered in a beard and a few days' worth of dirt. It took me weeks to track him down. The dead man in Kingston had no identification. My intelligence contacts recognized him from other jobs. I found a bank account that had a deposit from the man sprawled at my feet.

I grasp one meaty hand. The pinky. That's where I start. "How many fingers does one need?"

"Fuck," he cries. "I have no idea what you're talking about."

"Ten thousand dollars. Not the most expensive hit you've ever ordered. I suppose you thought a young woman with no guards would be easy."

"She had you," he snarls, giving up the pretense of ignorance.

It's a small crack, the break of his pinky finger. I don't feel particularly guilty. He has nine more. At least, he will keep the rest if he tells me what I want to know. The acrid scent of piss rises in the air. "That's right. She had me."

My phone vibrates, and I take it out. Only two people have this number. My brother Elijah, who I left running the business. It's my other brother Josh. My heart thuds. I give a hard twist to the index finger in my hand and feel the bones give way. A sharp scream rents the air. I drop the man to a puddle of writhing agony and step into the small kitchen to take the call.

"Hello?"

"Checking in," Josh says in a drawl. "Per your

request. The theater is secure. It's pretty close to a damn fortress already. I'm working with the local security team on some upgrades."

That does nothing to temper the feral part of me. It hurls its body against the bars, enraged that it can't be close to Samantha. "How is she? Did she start practicing?"

"Yes."

"Yes? That's it?"

"What do you want me to say?"

"Is she eating okay?"

"Jesus Christ. I'm not her nanny. I'm a body-guard."

If he's left her side for one second… "Close security means you should fucking well know what she's eating. This threat to her isn't a goddamn joke."

"I'm doing my job, asshole. You want to know what she's eating? You want to know how much she's sleeping or how practice is going, ask her yourself."

The line clicks off.

I put my hands on the cracked Formica countertop and hang my head. It feels wrong to be this far away from Samantha Brooks. Before she came into my life, I answered to no one. Not even my brothers. Now I can barely go twelve hours without getting an update.

She was in my custody for six years. I did my duty. I paid whatever debt I owed. It should be enough to know that she's safe. Her music haunts me. The sound of the bow against the strings, playing over and over in the room next to my office. A few weeks of silence since she left, and I'm about to go insane.

Well, not complete silence.

The man behind me babbles something nearly incoherent. I don't find myself with much mercy for someone who would order a hit on an innocent girl, even if she were a stranger. But Samantha? I want to rip him apart. Whether he talks or not, I want his blood sprayed across the goddamn wall. That's what he would have done to her. That's what he ordered done.

I haul him up against the wall. His eyes are wild and bloodshot. How much of the money he got for ordering her hit did he use to buy cocaine? That wild animal inside me wants to rip him apart with my bare hands. It's the cold, calculating exterior that speaks.

"A pinky isn't that useful, not unless you're going to fucking tea. Index finger, same thing. But your middle finger? Your forefinger? You ever want to finger a woman again? I don't imagine you get a lot of pussy based on your charm."

"What do you want from me?"

"Tell me where Alistair Brooks is, and I walk away." Against every instinct in my body.

He glares at me, pissed off because I've won. Well, he can join the club. I'm pissed off that this sack of shit is going to live. "He isn't in Russia, if that's why you're here."

Which means someone tipped him off. "Where?"

A small, gruesome smile with bloody teeth. "Back in the United States. In Tanglewood."

CHAPTER TWO

*A study published in The Journal of Hand Surgery found that
18 percent of people aren't born with the ability to
independently move their ring and pinky fingers in the way
needed to play violin at an elite level.*

SAMANTHA

I CLOSE MY eyes and let the notes wash over me.
Ten thousand hours of playing in the music
room at home can't compare to the acoustics in
the Grand. Everyone arrives tomorrow, which
means I'll have to share the practice space with a
tenor and a soprano and dancers, but right now
there's only me. An entire stage, a thousand red
velvet seats, five stories of open air. Only the
music I can make.

That's when I hear it, the smallest scuff that
did not come from my violin.

Blood pulses faster through my veins. Is it
Candy? She usually comes from backstage. This
sound came from the seats, far enough away that
the person is hidden. I squint into the farthest

corners of the floor level. Nothing moves.

It could be Josh, who spends most of his time sitting in the corner of the front row. He does a patrol every hour. Overkill, since nothing even remotely dangerous has happened. No one even knows I arrived in Tanglewood early.

Then again, maybe someone found out.

"Stop overreacting," I whisper.

It can be paralyzing to think of someone out there trying to kill me. A nameless, faceless someone—with a gun. So I don't let myself think about it. I let the bow fall to the strings, pressing a long C-note into the air. The violin wants to play, so I let it take the lead. I let it play the song to its end.

Clap. Clap. Clap.

Someone's clapping in the very back, slow and loud.

A man steps from the shadows at the back of the theater, tall and lean with gleaming golden hair. Even from this far away, without having ever met him in person, I know who this is. My muscles unclench in slow degrees. It isn't someone with a gun trying to kill me. No, this is the celebrity tenor headlining our tour. He has every right to be in this theater—more than me, in fact.

"That was beautiful," he says in that rich

chocolate voice, while his long legs eat up the red velvet carpet. He's wearing a grey suit that hugs his body and a white dress shirt open at the throat. "Your reputation doesn't do you justice, which is saying something."

All of the peace I'd felt on this stage, the certainty that I was in the right place, evaporates. I stand up, holding my violin and bow. It's like I'm six years old again, trying to explain to my father why I needed to practice late into the night. Being a child prodigy didn't make that go away.

"Harry March," I say, trying to sound casual. "Nice to meet you."

"Oh, I'm sure it is." He steps onto the barricade that surrounds the orchestra pit and takes a graceful leap to the stage. Every muscle in my body seizes until he lands safely on the other side. If he'd missed it would have been a twelve-foot drop. "This is the part where you giggle and toss your hair over your shoulder."

I blink at him. "Why would I do that?"

He grins. A shock of blond hair falls artfully across his forehead. The whole of him looks sculpted, someone's fantasy come to life. Unfortunately, it's not my fantasy. "That's what all the girls do. You, on the other hand, look annoyed that I'm interrupting your practice. I like that."

A reluctant smile curves my lips. "You're a flirt."

"And you're... taken, I'm guessing. Boyfriend? Fiancé? Are you married?"

"I'm only eighteen."

"The classical music world moves fast. Faster than Hollywood even."

That's actually true. Something about being a child prodigy, about working the kind of hours we do—there's a tendency to marry early. Besides, it doesn't have to be true love. We're married to our instruments more than people. At least, that's how it usually is.

"I'm not with anyone," I say, the words thick on my tongue. Being in love with a man doesn't count. He was my guardian, and briefly—so briefly it sometimes feels like a dream—my lover.

"Oh good," he says, flashing a mischievous smile. "I thought you might be with that strapping security guard out front. I left my entourage with him. In that case, you and I can have plenty of rebound sex to help you get over whoever it is you left behind."

"Do women actually say yes to this?"

"I find the direct approach gets us to the destination faster."

The direct approach. That sounds like the

exact opposite of anything I've done before. My feelings for my former guardian are complex and circuitous, winding around landmines of gratitude and protection and the forbidden nature of my desire. "No, thank you. But I appreciate the offer."

He puts a hand to his heart. "Wounded."

"I thought you weren't coming until tomorrow."

"I wanted to scope out the venue before the competition, but you're already one step ahead of me."

"We're not competing."

"Aren't we? The audience can only prefer one of us."

"Then it will definitely be you."

He laughs. "And modest. I find myself charmed and determined more than ever for us to have some of that rebound sex. Or is it revenge sex you'd prefer? We can upload the sex tape to YouTube."

I study him. "You know what? I think you're bluffing."

"About what?"

"Everything."

"Let me take you to dinner."

"I already have plans."

"Then take me with you."

It's with great reluctance that I actually consider his request. I'm going to see Bea, another performer on the tour. He'll have to meet her eventually, and I'm sure she'd appreciate an early glimpse of our resident celebrity. "Do you promise to behave yourself?"

"Of course I promise to behave myself. Abominably. That's why you'll bring me."

SAMANTHA

BEATRIX CARTWRIGHT AND I became friends long before our futures dovetailed together. The world of classical music is filled with grown-ups, most of them with white hair and stern expressions. Children were rare enough that we either became friends or lifelong enemies.

Thank goodness she never minded that I came from no musical background. And I never begrudged her loving mother who was a famous pianist. How could we know that years later we would both be orphaned? First a plane crash took her parents. Then my father died. Our emails to each other in the years that followed were a lifeline, a rare note of understanding.

"I don't understand you at all," Bea says,

glancing at Harry March, who looks radiant in the penthouse suite. The baby in her arms coos her agreement.

"It's not like I'm going to have sex with someone just because they're hot. Or because they're famous. Or because they ask. Though when I say it out loud, those do sound like good reasons."

"He's Harry freaking March."

"Exactly. Which means things would be super awkward after."

"You're probably right, but still, it's Harry freaking March." The man of honor stands with a crystal glass of some amber liquid, looking completely at ease and elegant against the silhouette of the city. Beside him Hugo pours himself a glass, wearing a suit that's less trendy, more classic.

I stick out my tongue at her, which makes the baby gurgle. "Come here, sweet girl." I accept the warm bundle of wriggly infant, breathing in deep. "I hope you don't mind that I brought him with me."

"Of course not. I'm not sure I'll be able to make the welcome dinner." Bea has come a long way from the sad voice in my inbox. She has a husband and a daughter, but her past still haunts her.

Her agoraphobia kept her locked inside this hotel for years. Only recently has she started venturing into the city. She will join the tour for the opening shows in Tanglewood, not the rest of it, and even that will be hard for her.

"We should have the dinner here."

She makes a face. "In my dining room? There's like twenty-five people."

"Downstairs. In the hotel restaurant. What's it called?"

"L'Etoile. It's got great food, but still…"

I take her hand and squeeze. "No one will mind. And, if they do, Hugo will punch them."

She manages a wan smile. "The truth is, I should have already been to the Grand. Candy offered for me to use the practice space or even to record videos there. They have a gorgeous grand. I've seen pictures."

A major record label put the tour together with different performers. Harry March is the most well-known, the headliner, but second to him would be Bea. She's built a massive following on YouTube by posting her covers to popular songs. The rest of us—the soprano and the gymnasts and myself—aren't known except in our small, professional circles.

"Do you think—" The baby fusses in my arms, and I return her to her mother, where she settles into sleep. "I'm sure you'll be able to when the time comes."

"Yes," Bea says, her voice dry. "Because leaving under pressure has worked before."

"One step at a time, but we're definitely moving the dinner to L'Etoile. I'll talk to the label rep so you don't have to. Don't even worry about it."

"Thank you," she says. "I appreciate it more than you know, but not so much that I'm going to let you off the hook about this Harry March thing."

"Ugh." I roll my eyes, even though it's fun to talk about a cute boy with someone. That's something that I missed, because I was busy pining over my guardian during my teenage years.

"Has he called?" she asks, her voice soft. She knows that we slept together. She also knows that I left him when he refused to open up—the man is determined to punish himself, and I got tired of being the horsewhip in that scenario.

"No calls. No emails. I didn't expect him to."

Bea is kind enough not to call me on the lie. The truth is that I did expect him to call or email. Or maybe send a carrier pigeon. It's been six years of almost constant contact. He was there every morning and every night. He was more than my guardian—he was the axis around which I spun.

CHAPTER THREE

The University of Breslau notified Johannes Brahms that he would receive an honorary doctorate in philosophy. Though he originally planned to write a handwritten note of acknowledgment, a friend convinced him protocol required him to write a musical offering. Thus, he wrote Academic Festival Overture, an irreverent compilation of student drinking songs.

LIAM

"WHAT DO YOU mean she's on a date?"

"I told you, I'm not her nanny. And I'm not your fucking spy. It's my job to keep her safe, which is what I'm doing standing outside the door."

"And if this fucker puts his hands on her?"

"Then she'll probably like it," my brother says, which makes me snarl across the thousands of miles. I should be more worried about the threat to her life. Or how she'll feel when she finds out her father's in the same city. And I am worried about those things. That doesn't stop me from wanting to punch the guy who might have his hands on her.

I'm on a private flight over the goddamn Atlantic Ocean. I can't do a damn thing about Samantha Brooks and whatever the pompous, privileged singer might be doing to her. That doesn't stop me from cursing my brother out in colorful and extremely violent terms.

He only laughs. "I said it before—you want to talk to her? You know her number."

The line clicks off, which makes me curse under my breath. I trust my brother enough to know he isn't going to let her get murdered on his watch. That doesn't mean she's safe. This Harry March asshole has a reputation, and Samantha is innocent enough to fall for him.

She's innocent because you made her that way.

Hell. I kept her protected from the world. Did that make her vulnerable? I should kick my own ass. I dial the numbers I've been avoiding for months now. When I press the last number my phone automatically pulls up Samantha's photograph. Her dark, fathomless eyes. Her silky chocolate hair. Those full lips turned up in an almost rueful smile. She's beautiful and unattainable for me, even knowing that I've had her in more ways than I should. She always deserved better than me.

I force myself to put the phone down.

The flight attendant moves around in the galley, wearing high heels that seem impractical ten thousand feet above ground. She bends over, and the male part of me wakes up.

This is what I deserve—a quick fuck with a stranger. What's her name? Honey, maybe. Or Haley. She walks down the aisle with a fresh drink. I take it with a nod of thanks. There are a handful of other seats on the private plane, each one leather and plush. I'm the only one here.

She smiles at me. "Is that your daughter?"

I look down at the smooth wooden table, where Samantha's photo is still on the screen. It's one of her senior pictures done by that company all the schools use. The background is some kind of hazy, generic blend of blue. She's not quite young enough to be my daughter, but it's close enough. Close enough considering I had custody of her for six years.

"No," I say, my voice hard.

The realization moves through the stewardess's eyes, from openness, from invitation. She would have let me fuck her... Then she begins to understand that I have this photo on my phone because I'm interested in a girl who was in high school only months ago. I let her think I'm that kind of a bastard, because it's the truth.

SAMANTHA

IT ISN'T HARD to convince the record label to move the welcome dinner to L'Etoile. A stuffy French restaurant fits the vibe of the tour perfectly. I wear an emerald green wrap dress with a gold necklace Liam gave me for my seventeenth birthday with a violin pendant. Nerves thrum beneath my skin, because I'm about to meet a lot of important people. People who could take my career to the next level. People who could tank my career, if they wanted to.

Josh insists he'll watch from the kitchen, where he can make rounds without disturbing anyone. Which makes sense, except that means I'm completely alone as I follow the maître d'.

The table is full of people, and it feels like hundreds of eyes turn toward me.

"Fashionably late," says a man in a suit with white hair. I vaguely recognize him from the record label, some higher-up administrative type of person.

"I'm not late," I say automatically, because I'm not. I'm not the kind of person to be late on purpose or to be late at all. That's something Liam's military punctuality drilled into me.

Seated at the head of the table, Harry March grins. "Dinner's at eight. Didn't you read the invitation?"

"That's not what mine said." It sounds like a lie, even to my own ears, but I can see the embossing in my mind. It said nine o'clock. My cheeks flame. "I must have read it wrong."

Bea stands and clasps my arm. "It doesn't matter," she says brightly, before whispering to me, "I think they put different times to mess with us. I should have checked ours."

"You couldn't have known," I whisper back.

At least I showed up before they ordered. I still feel ridiculous and fidgety. The only chair available is the one directly across from Harry March, as if I'm some guest of honor instead of simply the late one. *Fashionably late*, as the record label representative said. They think I'm a diva. Oh God, what if they think I'll be late for an actual show?

"Shall we go around the table and introduce ourselves?" Harry says, winking at me over the glasses of champagne and candles lighting the table. "For Samantha, of course."

My cheeks are probably two hundred degrees. Even my eyelids feel hot. "That's not necessary."

"Dierdre Hamilton," says the girl to the right of Harry, her blonde hair shiny, her skin pale as porcelain. Her red dress looks painted on her slender body. "The soprano."

That seems to be the cue for everyone else to go. There are three people from the record label, each with a job description I don't understand. The white-haired man is head of our account, whatever that means. There's a woman who doesn't look up from her phone when she mutters, "Tracy. Talent development." And a woman who somehow looks younger than me, who handles customer experience. "Staci with an I," she says with a bright smile.

Harry March introduces himself as, "*The* Harry March."

"Bethany Lewis," says a young black woman, her body sleek like an athlete, her eyes kind. "I'm from Cirque du Monde. It will be an honor to perform to your music. This is Romeo."

Romeo has tan skin and bold features. He raises one eyebrow at me, though I can't tell whether it's meant to be flirting or a challenge. Either way I'm vaguely intimidated.

The last person at the table is Bea, who gives me a playful wave. "Beatrix Cartwright. I've known you since we were six years old, and you let me borrow your Barbie's brush."

That makes me grin. We'd hidden in her mother's dressing room, mixing my Barbies with her troll dolls until we had enough to make a family. Even then we'd both been starved for a normal life. For a mother making dinner and a father teaching us how to ride a bike.

"Nice to meet you all," I say, meaning it. "I'm Samantha Brooks."

A man appears behind Harry, looking out of place with a scruffy beard and a baseball cap. "Sorry it took me a minute, folks. The asshole up front didn't want to let me back in without a tie."

"Oh, I should have mentioned that, too," Bea whispers.

The man picks up something large and black, and I realize it's a video camera. Like the kind you would see on a TV set. He swings it my way. "Say something, new girl."

"Hello," I say, feeling like I'm in a play without being given my script.

"Should we do the introductions again?" the customer experience person asks.

Bea shakes her head. "Definitely not. What is the film even for?"

"We're making a Netflix special," says Tracy of talent development, finally looking up from her phone. "Get to know the performers, behind the scenes, the making of a worldwide tour."

"I think we should be able to vote each other

off," Harry says, brown eyes twinkling.

Bethany looks uncomfortable. "I don't mean to be a pain, but has this been cleared with the agency? Our noncompete with Cirque is really strict. We only got clearance for the live shows."

"Legal's working it out," says the white-haired man. "And Harry has a point. One of the reasons we booked an extended rehearsal time is to increase the drama of the show."

"You mean you want us to fuck each other over," Romeo says.

"Or just fuck," Harry says helpfully.

Staci claps her hands to gather our attention. "This is not only our tour. It's *your* tour. We'd love to hear some of your ideas for how we can make it unique."

"Mud wrestling," Harry says immediately. "Samantha and Dierdre fight to the death."

Dierdre Hamilton rolls her eyes. "What if all of us had costumes done in only black and white, with a few pops of red? A performance isn't only about how it sounds. It's about how we look."

"A wet T-shirt contest," Harry suggests.

"We could all pick music from the same era," Bea says. "Like if we all played nineties pop music in acoustic ensembles, really exposed the soul of them."

"What if—" The entire table falls silent, and I curse myself for opening my mouth. The only thing to do now is follow through. "What if we did an Alice in Wonderland theme? The Grand has this amazing lighting system hidden in the recesses of the historic elements, and well, it was just a thought I had."

Harry raises an eyebrow. "Is this your way of getting me into a purple suit?"

"It's actually a good idea," the white-haired man says, the compliment ruined by his obvious surprise. "A theme is stronger than matching outfits or pop songs. Ms. Hamilton could play the part of Alice."

Harry snorts. "Because she has blonde hair? You lack imagination, George. Dierdre is way too jaded. No, she's clearly the Queen of Hearts. She'll make you bow and then cut off your head. And probably make you like it."

"It's true," Dierdre says, taking a sip of champagne.

"Bethany, then," George says.

"She has the innocence factor," Harry says in a musing tone. "But her performance is designed to partner with Romeo, isn't it? Alice in Wonderland isn't a love story. He can't be following her through the forest, unless you want to dress him up like a tree."

The words slip from me like a long exhale. "I wonder if the snow loves the trees and fields, that it kisses them so gently? And then it covers them up snug, you know, with a white quilt; and perhaps it says, 'Go to sleep, darlings, till the summer comes again.'"

Everyone stares at me, and my cheeks turn hot.

"Is that from Alice in Wonderland?" Bea asks, sounding impressed.

"Through the Looking Glass," I offer weakly. "I only thought of it because Harry said the thing about dressing up like a tree so they could dance."

"How many times have you read it?" Dierdre asks.

My heart thuds against my ribs. She thinks I could quote the book because I read it several times. Instead of once. For some reason my father always wanted to hide my memory. He said it was too showy for a little girl to have both violin mastery and a photographic memory. *Never tell anyone. It will be our little secret.* He's been gone a long time, but it still feels like something I'm supposed to hide.

"It should be Samantha," Beatrix says, saving me from answering. "She's the one who came up with the idea because she's the one who stepped through the looking glass."

My heart squeezes with fear and maybe a little bit of excitement. "No, it can't be me."

"You're the only one left," my friend says. "I'm only in the show in Tanglewood."

"But Alice is the star of the show. I only play the violin solo. It's one small part."

Harry leans forward, looking like the cat who got the cream. "All the more reason for you to be Alice. We'll be busy singing and dancing when you wander into the forest, lost and confused. And then your solo can be that piece you were playing at the Grand when we met."

A knot forms in my throat. That's my own composition, a song about loneliness. It's perfect for what he's describing, except that no one knows it exists.

Tracy suddenly looks interested. "What piece?"

She's expecting me to say Mozart or Beethoven. Maybe one of the modern composers doing experimental pieces, their black-and-white photographs gracing Playbills.

A soloist plays what she is given. It takes months, years of practicing some pieces before they're ready to perform. She can bring her interpretation to a piece, but composing is something else entirely.

I shove my chair back as the food arrives. "Excuse me, please."

The sight of steaks and oysters on heavy platters makes my stomach turn. I can't sit here with the black camera pointed at me and strangers deciding my fate.

Bea starts to get up, but I shake my head. "I just need some fresh air."

Maybe it's a low blow, but I know that will make sure she doesn't follow. She can leave the hotel these days, but it's still a big deal. I really do need some fresh air, though. Some fresh air where I'm alone, without eyes that see too much. Or maybe they don't see enough.

My thoughts turn to Liam. He would know what to say. It would be so simple for him. His brain was organized. He would sift through every possibility and come up with the right answer, without emotion. It was his greatest strength. His greatest weakness. And I miss him so much.

An ache spears my heart, and I stumble through the restaurant. Leaving is harder than I thought. Dark blue paneling lines the hallways, with little star lights embedded in them. It's like being lost in the galaxy, turning and twisting.

Finally I spy something different—thin double doors that must lead to the kitchen. I push inside, ignoring the way the waiters and cooks swear in surprise.

Josh stops me. "What the hell happened?"

"I'm getting some air," I say again, thinking they'll put that on my tombstone someday.

That's the difference between the two brothers. Liam would have made me explain what was wrong. He would have tried to fix it—and he probably would have succeeded. That's how he went through life. Taking command. Making everything better. Josh stepped back and let me pass.

A small patio had wrought iron tables and ivy-covered walls. A tall space heater was little proof against the chill of the night. I leaned back into the foliage, crossing my arms over my chest and closing my eyes. What's happening to me? I don't feel grown up enough to stand up for myself at that table, but I know I'm not a child. There's an agent in LA who looks over my contracts, but it's not the same thing as advice or guidance. It's not the same thing as Liam.

I feel someone block the breeze. It's Harry.

"Why did you follow me?" I ask, my voice unsteady.

"Why did you run?"

That's a simple question with a complicated answer. "Does it really matter? I'm going to do what the record label wants, and it sounds like you're the one calling the shots."

"Being the star of the show is a good thing for you."

I shake my head, not breaking eye contact. "I'm not the star."

One elegant shoulder lifts. "You make beautiful music. We can make beautiful music together."

My breath catches. As pickup lines go, it's not bad. "I like this better than the direct approach."

"But why do I have a feeling I'm still not getting laid tonight?"

"Why are you even out here with me when Dierdre Hamilton is at the table? Or is this some kind of publicity thing? Make the Netflix people think we're sleeping together?"

He snorts. "No. I don't fuck for money. Unlike your friend's husband."

My breath catches. Bea couldn't exactly date like a regular person when she couldn't leave the hotel. She finally hired a male escort to take her virginity. And ended up falling in love with him. Hugo is a good man. He doesn't exactly hide his past, but it would be a scandal if it became public knowledge.

"Now you're starting to understand," Harry says, resting one hand next to my head, leaning close. "Those record label people aren't here to keep us together. They're here to tear us apart. This tour is going to be headline news one way or another."

The words send a shiver down my spine.

LIAM

I THOUGHT I would approach her in a kind and distant manner, the way a father might check on his daughter at her first job. We would have a coffee. Maybe I would write her a check, something to ease the way. Everything would be civilized.

Isn't that what families do? I know fuck all about family.

And then I see her tucked into a dark corner, another man leaning over her. The tenor. The one who's on the tour with her. He's way too fucking close, and any hope of being civilized evaporates. I'm going on forty-seven hours without sleep. I didn't even have time to change after getting off the plane and taking a car here. I checked in at the front desk and then texted Josh, only to find out he didn't have eyes on her. *She wanted fresh air.*

What the fuck did that mean? It meant she was upset. So I'd dropped off my duffel bag in the room and come to look for her, except Harry fucking March is pushing his hips against her.

My heavy palm lands on his shoulder, and I squeeze until he yelps. "Pardon me," I say, my voice rough as a pile of rocks. "I believe this dance is mine."

I'm only distantly aware of him leaving. Then I'm looking down at Samantha, my throat locked tight. We aren't dancing, but it feels like I'm lost to her music.

"Liam?" she gasps, her eyes wide.

Maybe she's pissed that I ruined her private moment. Tough luck. "You let him touch you? What if he hadn't stopped when you wanted him to, Samantha? There's no one around."

"Then I'm sure you would have broken his nose," she says.

I would have broken more than that. I'm still considering it. *Fuck.* She brings out the wild animal in me, the beast that doesn't care about laws or morality. She's mine, and I want the world to know it. I want them to smell me on her. They won't even look her way, once they catch the scent. It's not fair to her—that I push her away only to drag her back. It's not fair, but it's unshakable. A pattern worn deep into the grooves.

My head dips to breathe her in. "What are you doing out here?"

"What are *you* doing out here?" she demands, her dark eyes flashing.

"I don't know," I tell her honestly, and my voice sounds hollow. She looks so pretty in the moonlight. "But I couldn't stay away any longer." Maybe it would always be this way, her sailing away, me dragged along like an anchor she can't shake.

She swallows, faint shadows moving at her slender throat. "They're talking about having me do some kind of acting thing for the show, more than just playing."

"And you're nervous?"

"Of course I'm nervous. What if I screw this up?"

"You already know you can play. It's not about ego. From the minute someone put a bow and violin in your little hands you could play better than most professional musicians." I pause, brushing my lips against her hair, light enough that she can't feel it. It could be the brush of the leaves in the wind. It doesn't have to be a kiss.

"Now you have to do something you're not naturally good at."

A huff of laughter. "I knew you'd make it simple. Are you saying I've had it easy?"

"The way you play isn't easy, not even for you—but you know you're the best in the world. Are you the best actress in the world? The best performer? No, but you'll be fucking amazing." She feels fucking amazing in my arms. Enough that I can't stop myself from leaning close, from pressing her along the length of my body. From pushing my erection against her stomach. I'm an animal. They shouldn't let me near her.

Her breath catches. "I missed you."

The words tumble out of her mouth, as if she can't hold them back. My heart clenches, a painful squeeze that reminds me of every second I've been apart from her.

One day I had been a man with a death wish—and the next I was responsible for a twelve-year-old girl. And then she grew up into a beautiful woman. At every turn she's been a surprise.

I touch my fingers to her temple and stroke her cheek. "If there's one thing I've learned in life it's that everything will change. Don't worry about your future. Do this because you love it, right now. Play. Compose. Perform. Sometimes all you have is right now."

My hand trails down her jaw, until the backs of my fingers rest against her throat. Her vocal cords vibrate as she speaks. Ripples of pleasure and pain resound through my body.

"I'm not performing right now," she whispers.

I have her tucked into the ivy, as deep as she can go. I'm blocking her with my body—keeping her within reach, keeping everyone else away. It's the only way I've ever been able to breathe.

A knot forms in my throat. "What do you want?"

Right now. The words move between us like the cool night breeze.

It shouldn't be possible for her to live up to the image in my head, the perfection that I've been imagining every goddamn night. Except it doesn't even do her justice.

She's living breathing perfection.

Somehow, I'm leaning close. Is it only me who wants this? Her breath brushes over my lips. "Right now, I want this," she whispers, and then she closes the centimeters between us.

Four weeks. That's how long I've been apart from her.

It might as well have been four years. A lifetime of silence. The moment her lips touch mine I'm suffused with music, thousands of notes that she's played for me, a million heartbeats.

By the time she pulls back I'm breathing hard. I can run a marathon barely breaking a sweat. Being near this woman is enough to break my body into pieces.

"Right now," I say, my voice unsteady.

"That's all we have." Her eyes search mine. "Or is there more?"

"You need to get back. They'll be waiting for you."

Disappointment darkens her pretty face. "Yeah, and somehow I was late. I swear my invitation didn't say anything about a cocktail hour before dinner. God, I wonder if they did that on purpose. Harry said they want us to have drama so we get more press."

"You're a world-class musician, Samantha. They can go to hell. Besides, we have bigger problems to worry about. Like the fact that you're still in danger."

A soft intake of breath. "How do you know?"

Because I tortured a man until he pissed himself. That's something she doesn't need to know. "It doesn't matter. The intelligence is good. That's the important part. So no going outside without Josh. I'm going to have a talk with him."

"Liam," she whispers. "Why are they doing this?"

"Because I have a responsibility to you. They know that. So they'll use you to draw me out. You would be bait, to get revenge on almost killing your father."

A notch forms between her eyebrows. "Who would avenge him?"

"He would. Your father isn't dead, Samantha."

A ripple of shock moves through her body. I wish I could shield her from it, but I take a step back instead. She's going to face this particular truth on her own. How can I help her when I'm the reason he should have died? When I'm the reason he's still alive?

"You're wrong," she says, her voice rough.

"I thought that fucker was sent to kill you, but you know what I think now? He was sent to kidnap you. You would be bait to bring me out of hiding."

Her eyes shine with unshed tears. "I don't understand."

Ancient pieces of my heart rattle, where ordinary human emotion would usually go. I want to take away all of her worries. I want to kill her father the way I should have years ago. Until six months ago I believed I had succeeded. I left a young girl alone in the world, and that guilt led me to take custody of her. It was a terrible domino effect—her father's duplicity, my assassination of him, my guardianship of Samantha.

"Understand this," I tell her. "Your father is not a good man."

She shakes her head, which isn't to disagree. It's more about being overwhelmed. "You know what? Fine. I believe you wouldn't have tried to kill him without cause. That still doesn't explain why you're here. Isn't that what they want? Luring you out?"

"I can take care of myself."

A snort. "Yes, the powerful Liam North doesn't need anyone."

"I came to warn you. To make sure you understand the stakes."

"Oh, I understand them." She sounds a little sad. Mostly resigned. "I'm starting to think you have a hero complex. You don't want to be with me? Then don't worry about my life."

That's the last thing she says to me before returning to the restaurant.

A hero complex? That's ironic, considering

I've never been anyone's hero. Definitely not Samantha's. That's something she's going to find out before this is over. Then again, part of her may already know. I think she remembers more than she wants to admit. That powerful memory of hers—she tries to hide it, for reasons I've never understood.

CHAPTER FOUR

Schubert wrote more than 600 songs in his brief life. Between
his first in 1811 and his last in 1828, he averaged three
every month.

SAMANTHA

POOF. THE DAYS of solitude and solemn
practice disappear in a cloud of smoke.

Now there are directions being shouted and
nails being hammered. The Grand has hosted
some major productions, but none have required
the kind of acrobatics that Bethany and Romeo
are going to do.

Thin silver lines need to hang from various
points on the ceiling. Strong enough to hold two
bodies. Discreet enough not to ruin the historic
lines of the building. There's also the little matter
of security upgrades that Josh insists on, and soon
a fine layer of dust hangs in the air.

Water pools in my lower lashes, and I twitch
my nose to avoid sneezing. Again.

The cameras are less intrusive than I thought

they would be. They're set up at various points in the theater, with men in grubby T-shirts and baseball caps who check on them periodically. They're not putting them in our faces, so it's easy to forget they're there.

Tracy the talent manager has us run through a skeleton set five times before we can take a break. It seems like Staci's job is to stand next to her, shouting out encouraging things like, "You're working so hard," and "Almost there!" that somehow make me feel worse.

When Tracy ends up in an argument with Romeo about the proper form for a backflip, I sneak offstage. There are dressing rooms behind the stage. That's where I find Beatrix, lying down on one of the plush vintage sofas, her baby sleeping soundly in her arms.

I tiptoe close to them and sit down on the floor, my back against the sofa, not wanting to wake them. They look so peaceful. And at the same time, prepared for some catastrophe. Of all people, Bea understands how quickly fortunes can change.

How vulnerable a child can be in the world. Vulnerable, if someone attempts to assassinate your only parent and you take a sip of the poison. Vulnerable, if you don't have anywhere to go—

and the only man who's willing to take care of you is the one who nearly killed you. So very vulnerable, if your father wants to use you as bait to get revenge.

"Hey," she says, her voice soft and drowsy, her eyes closed. "Are they still running the rehearsal like some kind of military insurgence out there?"

That makes me laugh. "Maybe we can invade France after lunch."

"You handled her well."

Everyone has gotten into an argument with Tracy, and it's not even 11 a.m. I might have been the exception. Her drill sergeant tone doesn't bother me, thanks to growing up around ex-military men and women at the compound.

Except she'd tried to stop Bea from nursing the baby, and I'd seen red. "I don't think she's going to be developing my talent."

"Well, Madeline appreciates your talents. And if she hadn't gotten milk she would have given the entire construction crew out there a demonstration of the acoustics."

My forefinger touches the clenched baby fist. "I don't want to wake her up."

"You can't," Bea says, a little rueful. "She's drunk on milk and cuddles right now. Nothing could wake her up for the next thirty minutes or so. If only it could last through the night."

"Do you need help? Maybe I could sleep over."

"No way. You're a single girl living in the city for the first time. There is no way I'm making you change diapers when you should be going out to clubs."

"I'm not going to any clubs," I say, laughing.

"Well, you should." Her dark red lashes touch her freckled cheeks. "Though I have a favor to ask you. A big favor, actually. We want you to be Madeline's godmother."

My breath catches. "What?"

"We have her godfather picked out already. Sutton. He's a good friend of Hugo's, but I just thought… I know you're still young and probably don't want the responsibility, but—"

"I'll do it. Of course I'll do it."

"I already think of you like family. And even though it's mostly a ceremonial thing, I know that you understand how important it is—even the possibility of losing us."

A clench in the vicinity of my heart. "Yes."

"And anyway, there's no one I trust more than you."

"You're going to make me cry," I say, but it's too late. There's already a burn behind my eyelids.

"She'll always be able to count on me, Bea. I promise you that."

"I already know."

Ten tiny fingers and ten tiny toes. I love that Beatrix is a mother, but I can't imagine ever doing it myself. Always wondering if the next twist of fortune's wheel would leave my child alone. It wouldn't even matter what happened to me. The world is a scary place for a child with no parent.

"So, remember how I told you Liam came to the dinner?"

"You mean he crashed the dinner."

"He didn't even come inside the restaurant." My heart clenches at the memory. Liam North made the world less scary for six years.

It's been two weeks since he crashed the dinner. There's been no sign of him. I don't know if he's still in the city or if he went back home. He could be a thousand miles away, but I feel his nearness. It pulls me toward him as sure and strong as gravity.

And somewhere else in the city is my father.

"Anyway, he told me something that's kind of crazy. Remember how I told you about the poison? How Liam had put some in my father's coffee and I'd gotten sick."

"Yes, though it's hard to believe Liam would

ever hurt a child."

"That part was an accident. He saved me that night, and in doing so, didn't make sure my father was really dead. Now he thinks my father is still alive."

Pale green eyes widen. "Oh my God."

"I know. It's impossible, right? It has to be."

She shakes her head slowly. "I don't know. But it does seem like—"

"Like what?"

"This could be your chance to find out what really happened. To ask your dad about the things that Liam accused him of. Demand answers. You deserve them."

"You think Liam made it up?"

"No, but I think he's human. He's fallible. He could be wrong. And the truth is he played judge, jury, and executioner back then."

"It's not like I can pick up the phone and ask my father. Besides, he's the reason I'm in danger. He wants to use me as bait to get revenge on Liam."

"How do you know?"

"I mean, that part makes sense. It's the only reason he would want to see me now, after all this time. He hasn't contacted me for six years. He let me think he was dead."

"That's true. But you were living with Liam North, the man who tried to kill him. He may have felt like he couldn't contact you without exposing himself. Now you're in Tanglewood. On tour. Maybe he wants to see you."

Hope stirs in my chest, wrong and irrepressible. I'm not sure there's an orphan in the world who wouldn't secretly want to see her father again. Even if her father was someone who betrayed his country. "Do you think so?"

"I honestly don't know, but if there was a chance my father was alive, I wouldn't be able to rest until I found him. I can't imagine how you're staying so calm."

"I'm afraid."

"Do you trust Liam?"

"Of course I do, and that's the problem. He's turning the theater into Fort Knox, but it's not like I'm going to live here forever. We're going to be traveling around the country. Around the globe. If my father's really trying to reach me, he'll have a million chances."

LIAM

I'M SITTING IN the very last row on the highest balcony. The nosebleed section. From this far away Samantha should be a speck of dust—barely recognizable as a young woman playing the violin. Except I can see every breath she takes. Every shadow at the base of her throat. The construction crews and the rest of the tour people fade away. She's the only thing I can see.

Movement of air. That's the only sign that I'm no longer alone.

I make a show of looking at my watch. "Took you long enough, little brother."

"That's fucking low," Josh says. "Even for you."

"It's always the human element."

At this moment there's a guard racing across the city because his wife is in labor. At least that's what he thinks. It was easy enough to tap into her phone while she breathed through her Lamaze class and send a text. *My water broke. The car won't start.*

Rotation schedules and simulations, state-of-the-art equipment and facial recognition software. Money can buy the best security, but the weakest link will always be humans.

Josh sits down next to me, slouching because he knows it annoys me. "Yeah, in this case the human element is that my brother's an asshole. Forgot to mention that to the men in the daily briefing."

"I saw you staring at the pretty gymnast. It took you twenty minutes to find me. The human element isn't the man with the pregnant wife. It's you."

He slouches lower, which is how I know I've made my point. "You're the only one who gets past my security, which means Samantha is safe with me. From everyone except you."

"Probably, but do you want to stake her life on that?"

"You really think he's going to try something?"

"No, I just like breaking into concert rehearsals as a hobby."

"Sure you do. As long as that rehearsal includes Samantha Brooks."

Her bow moves over the strings, making a sweet note soar through the air, impossibly clear, terribly poignant even from the back row. "I really do think he's going to try something."

"He's been in hiding all this time. What changed?"

"I don't know." And I hate not knowing. I hate not being able to protect Samantha with my own body, to place myself between her and harm's way.

Harm is hiding in the shadows. Like me.

"He's pissed because you tried to kill him, though."

"Yes."

"So this is about revenge. Six years is a long time to wait."

"It could be he just found out about it. Or that he's been waiting for the chance all this time, that he's come into money and influence right now and he's using it to get what he's wanted for years. It took some doing to get into the country."

"Christ, Liam. How much is your guilt going to cost you?"

"What the hell do you mean?"

"You felt so guilty for that night you took in an orphan. You raised her for six years. Now you're going to follow her around on tour. Would you like to wear a hair shirt while you do it? Maybe flog yourself a few hundred times a night? It sucks she took a sip of that coffee. It wasn't something you could have predicted. Sometimes there's collateral damage in this business."

I was recruited into a black ops division soon after deployment. My marksmanship was enough to get me noticed, but it was my psychological profile that made me perfect. Endless patience and enough moral ambiguity to make killing people palatable. My brothers know enough about my division to guess what I did, but they never said it out loud. Until now.

"It wasn't only that she took a drink." I don't know why I'm explaining this. Maybe so he'll understand the threat against Samantha. Or maybe because it feels cleansing to tell another human being. "I wasn't ordered to kill him. I was ordered to stand down."

Josh raises his eyebrows. "He wasn't dirty?"

"Oh, he was dirty. I gathered the evidence and waited for the kill order. But he had friends in high places. I made a call that night, a personal call. Samantha was supposed to be performing at a recital. He would have been found dead before she even got home."

"So now you repent."

I could have stayed where I was, making sure the man died like he was supposed to. It's what the traitor deserved. It's what I would have done, if the orders had come down like they usually did. It would have meant watching an innocent little girl die, too.

They may call it special ops and even give me fucking medals, but I was an assassin. A cold-hearted assassin, but even I couldn't do that. So I carried her to the hospital, where they saved her life. I killed so many people, but she was the first one I saved.

"Ten people," I say, my voice hard. The doctor who pumped her stomach. A nurse. The maid who helped me smuggle her back into the house. Two members of the *politsiya*. A handful of others who know about the violin prodigy who almost died that night. In saving her I also risked myself and my country. I risked everything for Samantha Brooks, and if I could do it over, I would again.

"Eleven," Josh says. "If you weren't counting Alistair Brooks."

No, I wasn't. He was supposed to be dead. There was enough poison in the coffee to do the job. I watched him drink it and vomit on the desk and pass out. But I didn't watch him die. I was busy carrying Samantha out of the room. Who helped him? Someone did.

I don't have to wonder why he pretended to be dead. He knew someone tried to kill him. I'm only wondering why he's trying to come out of hiding now.

"Have you ever thought about letting him find her?"

My blood runs cold. "The fuck?"

"A thousand people are going to walk through those doors in about a month. And then another thousand the next night. And the next."

"Then we screen every single one of them."

"You're forgetting something."

"What's that?"

"We might be able to stop him from getting to her, but what if she goes searching for him? She might want to find her long-lost daddy. I won't be able to stop her."

"The human element," I say, my voice grim. It's always the weakest link. She doesn't know her father was a traitor, and I'm not sure it would stop her even if she did. "I told her he's fucking dangerous."

Does she believe me? It might not be enough.

Down on the stage the representative from the record label points to a place on the stage. Samantha goes to stand there. The two gymnasts do some sort of swooping swan dives on invisible string, narrowly missing her. Smooth brown strands of hair rustle with the near miss.

She's definitely doing more than playing the violin.

They have her playing a part, this Alice in her musical Wonderland. She eats a cake and grows ten feet tall on risers. She drinks from a cup and shrinks back to normal size.

There's a key to the door just out of reach.

CHAPTER FIVE

As a child, the composer Joseph Haydn cut off the pigtails of a fellow choir member as a practical joke.

SAMANTHA

"YOU'RE ALWAYS SO serious," Harry complains. "You know how to play the violin, but you don't have any idea how to really *play.* How to be playful. How to have fun."

"I know how to have fun," I say, but that's mostly a lie. I know how to make a joke with the notes, a stop and start, a reversal of expectations—the kind of playfulness only understood by professional musicians. He's talking about something else. About showmanship. He's talking about being a clown for the audience, and that's something I definitely don't know how to do.

"We aren't a circus." A small defiance.

"No." He snorts. "We're ten times more expensive than any circus. So we need to be ten times better. That doesn't mean put them to sleep."

I manage not to flinch, but it's a close thing. Put them to sleep? I've trained for years. For decades, learning every nuance of timing and position. All of it fades in comparison with my ability to prance and trip onstage, acting like the fumbling Alice in her tragic Wonderland.

"I'll do it again," I say, picking up my violin. The piece is Brahms. Thankfully Harry let the idea of my original composition drop. "Playful this time."

Harry doesn't look appeased. He looks annoyed. "Fine. Whatever."

"I said I'd try again. At least I'm practicing. I haven't even heard you sing."

"In this mess." He waves a hand at the construction crew working onstage. "I can't even hear myself think, and I'm sure as hell not sawing my vocal cords open with this dust."

I hug my violin close to my chest. Lady Tennant is a Stradivarius, worth an insane amount of money and insured against damage or theft. Though I don't want her harmed by the dust.

"It's late anyway," I say, moving to the violin case.

"Yes. Late. We should get the fuck out of here." Harry seems to be in a strange mood, but then he's like this every day. Laughing one second and brooding the next. Mercurial.

"See you tomorrow," I say, running a velvet cloth over the wood. There's a process to putting the violin away. It soothes me as much as it does Lady Tennant.

"Fuck," he says. "I'm sorry."

I glance back at him after I click the brass lock closed. "For what?"

"For being an asshole. What else? Come on. Let's get out of here."

My eyebrows rise. "Out of here?"

"Go for a drive. Explore the city. We've been trapped in this godforsaken theater. Didn't they think we should see something of Tanglewood while we're here."

It actually does sound good to see the city. The limo takes us to the Grand and then back to the hotel. Practice is twelve hours a day, with the banging and the shouting nonstop. Dierdre has a lot to say to the white-haired record label executive. "I can't."

"Because your babysitter will lose his shit?"

Because maybe my father is alive. What does it mean? I have no idea how it's possible. I was in the room when he died. I may not remember the details—I blacked out from the shock and the grief of it—but I know that we had a funeral. His death was on CNN. A knot forms in my throat. "Maybe my babysitter has a good reason for worrying about my safety."

"I get twelve death threats a minute, sweetheart. You don't see me walking around with a personal bodyguard or asking for them to modify a historic fucking building."

"Maybe you should," I shoot back. "What does it hurt to be careful?"

"What does it hurt? How about living? Come with me, little violin prodigy. I want to take you into the looking glass, the real one that happens in Tanglewood after dark."

"What does that mean?"

"It means you're going to get something to drink."

I look away from those challenging brown eyes. Liam would be furious if he knew I was even considering this. Then again, I haven't seen him since the night at L'Etoile. The night he crashed the dinner party and dropped the bomb about my father, as if I wouldn't have a thousand questions. How do you know? Have you seen him? When did you find out he was alive? The possibilities bounce around my head, leaving me dizzy in their wake. I find myself looking at the back of every construction worker who passes through here, every security professional who works on the tech system. It's like I'm expecting these random men to turn around and suddenly my father will be there.

Which is insane. "Okay, I'll get something to drink."

Harry's eyebrows rise. "Really? I expected you to say no."

How sad. Beatrix was right. I'm a single girl in the city for the first time. I should be out having a good time or whatever eighteen-year-olds do. "Where will you take me?"

"I'm not sure if I'll get another shot, so we're going to the best place. The Den."

"The Den?"

"There's a bar and a dance floor, but it's not really a club. It's more like one of those old-world gentleman clubs. A parlor where people debate ideas and smoke cigars."

"And you want to debate ideas?"

"God no. I go for the bar and the dancing."

It's surprisingly easy to convince Josh. We pile into the back of a limo, the three of us. I'm not sneaking through the gate this time. I have my bodyguard. I'm taking precautions. There's absolutely no reason for Liam to come swooping in to scold me again.

The strange part is that I want him to.

SAMANTHA

"WHAT'S SHE DOING here?" Josh says, loud enough for everyone to hear.

We're standing in the glittering foyer of the Den. The heavy chandelier above us and beveled mirrors on the walls give everyone a magical quality. Harry hands his jacket to a valet who disappears with it. A cameraman for the Netflix show accompanied us in the limo. At least he's too busy fiddling with the many buttons on the camera to pay attention to Josh.

There are a few other men arriving at the same time, but the only other woman is Bethany, the gymnast from Cirque du Monde. She's wearing a little black dress, but it seems like she always looks like an Amazon warrior. It's the arms, I think. They're slender but clearly so strong.

"Shhh." I elbow Josh in the side. One of the benefits of growing up with your bodyguard is that I can hurt him when he's being an asshole. "She can hear you."

"Good." Josh's eyes are a darker green than Liam's, almost black.

They flash like onyx, as if he's furious. Which

is weird for a lot of reasons. Starting with the fact that Josh almost never gets mad. In fact he never has strong feelings about anything. And ending with the fact that Bethany's the most unoffensive person in the concert.

She keeps her head down and works hard.

"What is your deal? Everyone comes here." They make little jokes about things that happened the night before. That's mostly why I agreed to come. Dierdre mostly keeps to herself, but even she goes out with them. All I've wanted is to belong, and for better or for worse, the people on this tour are my family. At least for the next year and a half.

"Whatever," he mutters, unaccountable anger rolling off him in waves. "I'm going to have a little chat with the security team. Or what passes for it here."

He storms away, and I'm left stammering an apology. "God, I don't know what got into him," I tell her, though she doesn't meet my eyes. "I'm sorry."

"It's okay," she says, but it really isn't okay.

"He probably wants to fuck you." Harry rolls up his sleeves as if he's about to do something strenuous. Maybe he does the drinking and the dancing hard enough to be strenuous.

Bethany gives a soft laugh. "I don't think so."

"You should," Harry says, sounding completely serious. "Hate sex is the best sex."

I make a face. "That's not even a thing."

Everyone in the foyer looks at me. Even the super discreet valet gives me a glance. "Oh, my sweet summer child," Harry says, shaking his head, a gorgeous grin on his dumb, condescending face. "My innocent little lamb. My clueless, naïve—"

"Okay," I say, my voice a little strangled. Is the cameraman catching this? "I get it. I don't know anything about anything. Can we go inside and get a drink or something?"

Thankfully the mention of a drink convinces everyone to stop staring at me. I follow them inside to a large ballroom with a gleaming bar at the end. Harry heads straight there, leaving Bethany and me in the doorway.

A woman with blonde curls sits on the last stool, a small crowd gathered around her—but kept at a respectful distance. She looks like a queen holding court.

"That's Penny," Bethany murmurs, apparently deciding to take pity on the new girl despite her asshole of a bodyguard. "She runs this place, along with her husband, Damon Scott."

SKYE WARREN

There's a pause where I think I'm supposed to recognize the name. "Is he coming to the concert?"

She laughs, though not in a mean way. "Yes, I'm sure he'll be there in the most expensive box seats. He's some kind of shady but super rich businessman."

Now I'm feeling very out of the loop. "How do you know all this? Is there some kind of newsletter I can subscribe to, to learn about the different kinds of sex and powerful people?"

"I get most of my information from Romeo," she says, apologetic.

"Oh. Are you two… an item?"

"God no. We're like siblings. Plus, he's gay."

"I really am sorry about Josh. I have no idea what got into him. I mean he's an asshole, but usually it's more in a funny way."

She sighs. "That's okay. I already knew he didn't like me."

"When did he even meet you?"

"Oh, he's always sauntering around the theater. Checking the exits and stuff. I think they have that place locked down tighter than Fort Knox." She pauses. "Do you have a stalker or something?"

Ensconced in the safety of the Grand it's been easy to let go of the fear, but it comes rushing

68

back in a full body shiver. "Something like that."

"I figured that's why you never came out with us at night."

The room is packed with men in suits and women in skintight dresses, with ten thousand-dollar watches and multifaceted diamonds. This is a wealthy crowd, but that doesn't mean it's a safe one. "That wasn't why. I'm just really… introverted. And shy. And terrified of people."

She smiles. "Some profession you picked."

"Tell me about it. All I really want to do is play the violin."

"You know I used to think that about movement, about dancing and the rope work. That I would do it in a quiet, dark room forever if I could get paid for it. Then I realized there's something about the audience that feeds my creativity. There's an energy almost like a conversation."

"That sounds amazing, the way you put it. I have to be honest, I haven't performed in front of an audience in years. I don't know why I even got invited to this tour."

"Don't you?" She looks at me funny. "Harry March basically demanded it. That was the only way he agreed to do the tour, if they booked you too."

CHAPTER SIX

Shostakovich composed Tahiti Trot in less than an hour after making a bet for vodka. He hated the piece.

LIAM

THE TEXT COMES when I'm sitting in the private study of Damon Scott. There's absolutely nothing on his desk. No lamp. No papers. No laptop. It emphasizes the fact that he deals in information—passed from mouth to mouth. There won't be any paper trail, because there's no paper.

Tag, you're it. The words flash across my phone. Frustration tightens my jaw. I want to ignore it, but my little brother does not make idle threats. The stakes are too high.

I type back three question marks and hit *Send*.

"Something wrong?" Damon says, his voice overly polite. This isn't a man accustomed to being made to wait. His fingers drum the desk. The smooth surface of the wood gleams, broken only by a few deep, blackened gouges.

"No." I force myself to put the phone aside, when what I really want to do is call Josh. What the hell does that mean? *Tag, you're it.* My insides shred every second I'm away from Samantha.

"And so you want me to find out where this Alistair Brooks is hiding in the city… for how much money?"

"I suggested you do it out of the goodness of your heart," I say, my tone dry. "Though I'm prepared to pay. If you do more than tell me. If you deliver him to me."

Humor flashes silver-quick across his face. "Maybe this Brooks could pay me more to deliver *you* to *him*. I am a businessman, after all. And this is a free market."

My phone lights up. *You're at the Den tonight, right?*

Do not bring her here, I text back.

We're on our way.

DO NOT BRING HER HERE.

Christ. I force my attention back to the conversation in the room. What the hell were we talking about? Oh right. My death. "You're a businessman, but also a man of your word. At least that's what I was told."

"By whom?"

"Blue Eastman." I've gotten friendly with the head of security at the Grand. He'll probably forgive me for the little stunt I pulled on him.

"Ah. Him of the many cherubic infants at home."

"I wouldn't know."

Damon Scott leans forward, eyeing the phone with amusement. "Blue was right. I won't break my word. But there's one little problem. I haven't given you my word."

"Let me know when you do."

That's the last thing I say before I leave the room, taking my damn phone with me. I should probably have used more finesse. Damon Scott seems like the kind of man who can be charming. Persuasive. That's not me. I'm direct. I pay well and expect results. Which means I normally would have pressed him to make a decision. I can't think when I know Samantha is nearby.

I leave the office and stride through onto the main floor, ignoring the looks I get. Combat boots and a black T-shirt are far from the standard uniform here. Even the bouncers are better dressed.

There are at least three hundred people in the ballroom alone. I spot her immediately.

Her hair's in some sort of twisty up-do that I don't recognize. Did someone do that for her? Did she learn to do it in the past six weeks? There must be pins holding up the heavy mass. The curls overflow. They brush her neck. Her black dress is plain—and all the more striking in a roomful of bright color and sparkling jewels. She has always been stunning. My mouth goes dry.

Josh is nowhere in sight, but then I knew he wouldn't be. I'm going to kick his ass.

Samantha keeps to the edges of the room, watching, watching, watching. A man approaches her. I can only see broad shoulders in a suit from behind. She gives him a guarded smile and shakes her head. *No, thank you.* I can only take a breath when he walks away.

More men glance at her. The full-body glance. Wolves, all of us.

She circles the room until she finds a door cut into the paneling. With only a quick look over her shoulder, she disappears down a stairwell. I follow, but there's no choice involved. An invisible string connects me to her. I'm dragged along like a forgotten balloon.

The stairwell is narrow and musty, a throw-back to the days of servants and masters.

She walks with a casual curiosity down a dark-ened hallway. A peek into a room. Then she disappears. I follow her, watching through the sliver left in the doorway. Leather chairs and sofas form an intimate and empty audience. A grand piano rests on a raised platform.

Samantha sits down at the bench. Her hand runs over the ivory and black keys. She can play the piano with flawless and rare perfection. A side effect of being a prodigy. She can play anything. The violin was her choice.

Nimble fingers play a haunting tune that I recognize from that night long ago—her own composition. The bass thump-thumps above us, a heavy, modern beat, but she was made for this, for strings tuned to vibrate at nuanced frequencies, for a live audience.

Her body stills, and I recognize the awareness in the tilt of her head. She senses someone's here. That's a good thing. Those are the instincts that will keep her safe.

Her eyes meet mine, and she gasps. I must be only a pair of eyes in the shadow of the hall. Slowly I push open the door and step inside. Probably I should shepherd her upstairs and back to her hotel. Probably I should leave her sweet body alone. I close the door behind me.

Those beautiful brown eyes blink at me, mysterious, opaque. It would be a mistake to assume she's innocent, though. There's intelligence behind those eyes. A bone-deep current of survival.

And music.

She looks down at her hands as she plays something else. Beethoven's 5 Secrets. My breath catches. It's what she played for me the night I knelt at her feet. The night I tasted her pussy for the first time.

SAMANTHA

IT FEELS LIKE I conjured him from my thoughts.

He sits down in the leather chair front and center. My fingers fly over the smooth keys, playing faster and surer, finding their rhythm deep within the wood.

It's a string instrument, the piano, its strings hidden in its heart.

Anxiety holds me tense during rehearsals. I don't feel it now. It wouldn't come to me even if every leather seat filled up. The Grand has an incredible history and world-class acoustics, but this small stage… This is the way music should be shared, a modern, high-end version of a campfire.

A place for people to come together and tell stories.

That's what music is at its core—a story told in the universal language.

It's the way I tell Liam North how much I missed him, how angry I am that he stayed away for so long. It might be unfair of me. I'm the one who left. I don't care. He's my guardian. My protector, whether I'm twelve years old or eighteen. He should know that I needed him here.

Something flashes through his eyes. It isn't apology. *Recognition.* He hears my song. He understands what the notes mean, and that's the sweetest gift he could give.

Silence falls, swift and thick as rain. We're drenched in it. My hands lift from the keys. I stopped in the middle of the song. A crescendo. It wasn't the end. I couldn't play anymore.

I stand and cross the small stage. The platform is only two feet off the ground, but it may as well be a mountain for how far down he looks, reclined on the low leather seat.

"Where have you been?"

His voice is low. "The same places you've been."

"The hotel? The Grand? The limo taking me back and forth? Those are the only places I've been."

"You ate in the restaurant for breakfast. Oatmeal with brown sugar. Too much brown sugar."

"You're staying at L'Etoile?"

"The record label people are trying to change the way you stand, the way you hold the bow. They're trying to change the way you play. Don't let them."

I skip down to the ground level, where a plush carpet tilts my heels. My knees buckle. It's a close thing, almost falling on my face, but I manage to remain standing. He doesn't move a muscle.

He's so strong and virile in that chair, his skin darkened from the sun, a cut through his eyebrow that wasn't there before. What exactly was he doing in the six weeks since I left his house? Growth darkens his jaw. He looks disreputable, especially in such a luxurious setting. The kind of disrepute no one would question. The dangerous kind.

"They've recorded some of the best violinists alive. And some that are no longer alive. Maybe I should listen to them."

"You were born knowing, Samantha."

A kind of grief moves through my chest. I've never wanted to *not* be a prodigy. It's defined my life as much as being a woman, as much as having ten fingers and ten toes. I wouldn't know how to be anything else. "Doesn't that make it less real? That I showed up like this? What about hard work? Shouldn't that count for more?"

"You practiced for hours every day. You fought your father for the right to practice, to play into the night. He wanted to sell your violin. You had no rights, no power, but you fought him anyway. That counts for something. That counts for everything."

The space between us shrinks and shrinks, even when I'm standing still. There's nothing I can do but cross the few feet of carpet to him. Nothing to do but climb into his lap. A daughter might sit in her father's lap. I'm not his daughter. It isn't a child-like position, not when I throw my leg over his, straddling him. Not when I put my palms on his chest.

We could have sex in this position. I can feel him, hard and hot against the inside of my thigh. Even through the rough canvas of his pants.

"You don't want to touch me," he says, gruff, forbidding. Anyone else would back away. It's the growl of a wild animal, a warning sign that makes the hair rise on the back of my neck.

It makes me sink more fully around him. I press my forehead against his. God, I've missed this. Missed the closeness. Missed the surety. "I have no rights," I whisper. "No power. I'm fighting anyway."

A rough sound. "Fuck. *Fuck*. Samantha."

His breath caresses my lips. "You let me walk away."

"Good. You shouldn't be near me."

"This again? You're not my guardian anymore."

"That's not why. You shouldn't be near me. You *wouldn't* be near me if you knew what goes through my head, all the ways I want to defile you. I'd lock you up and keep you in the dark. I'd make you play for me until your fingers bled."

This man. The rawness of his voice tells me he speaks the truth—as far as he knows it. But I'm not scared of him. I can't be scared of him. He had ten thousand chances to hurt me.

I bend to his ear. "Prove it."

A flash of lightning. Not in the sky. It's a crackle in the air. I'm not expecting him to really do it, to prove anything to me. No, he will only demur. Only tell me I can't handle him. That I shouldn't be near him. The earth turns upside down. God, I should have known. He's always been a man of action.

He flips us so that he's over me, and I'm bent over the back of the armchair, clutching the broad padded panel, my ass turned up to him. His hips press against my ass. He speaks against my neck. "I kept myself in check because of your age.

Because you were my responsibility. My ward. They were chains around my wrists. Manacles on my ankles. They kept you safe."

I'm panting and uncertain—and I've never been more turned on in my life. I'm hot between my legs, already slippery for him. The animal part of me knows exactly what to do with this aggressive male: submit. Soft where he's hard. Slick while he's dying of thirst.

"Now those things are gone," he says, his voice almost conversational as he lifts my dress. Cool air whispers over my skin. He can see my panties right now. I'm staring at the brown leather, and he can see the place my panties are damp. "What will keep you safe now?"

For maybe the first time in my life, I don't want to be safe. I push my ass back, tempting him, begging him. "I don't know," I say, but they aren't words. They're a plea. I need him to do something, anything.

Crack. Pain spreads across my ass cheek.

Oh my God. He spanked me.

"That's for making my cock hard." He smooths away the sting with his palm. Two fingers slide my panties down. He touches the outer lips of my sex with a tortured groan. "That's also for making my cock hard. Everything I do, it's because you make my cock hard. How's that for being in control? I'm a grown man being led around by this tight little pussy. No matter where I am or what I'm doing, there's always part of me wanting inside you."

I shudder as he works two fingers into my core. I'm so swollen it feels like a stretch, even this much. There's an ache so acute it feels like a knife. "Liam. Please."

He finds a place inside me, and my mouth drops open on a silent scream. Above us there are hundreds of people dancing and drinking. I'm coming apart under their feet. His thumb brushes my clit, and my body bucks against his hand—once, twice. He pulls out and pushes in again, fucking me with the column of his fingers the way he'd do with his cock. Friction makes me moan. I hump the leather chair, rocking my hips, shameless, desperate for some kind of relief.

"That's right," he mutters. "Make yourself feel good. This is all you have. All you'll have if you chain yourself to me. Not a stage. Not a goddamn future."

I want to argue with him, but the climax crashes over me like a tidal wave. I close my eyes against the salt sting and ride it out in a tumult of emotion and pleasure. It leaves my body wrung out and lax. I wash up on the shore of that chair. I've been shipwrecked here. Adrift.

In that moment of aimless floating I have clarity. The question forms without any thoughts before it. *You practiced for hours every day. You fought your father for the right to practice, to play into the night. He wanted to sell your violin.*

"How did you know about the violin?" My voice sounds rusty as if maybe I screamed without knowing.

He smooths my dress down. "What violin?"

"The one I had when my father died." An expensive violin for a child. It was loaned to me by a nonprofit institute that cares about such things. We didn't own it. It would have been stealing to sell it, but it was worth a lot of money—and my father was continually broke.

I never told Liam North about my father threatening to sell the violin.

A sound comes from the door. Liam moves in a soundless rush. My heart pounds; we're vulnerable like this. Except he holds a gun pointing at the door. He isn't vulnerable, not even in this moment, and I have the hollow sensation of realizing that I was alone in my abandon. Liam North will not ever lose himself in me—that fact keeps me safe as much as it keeps him at a distance.

Harry March strolls inside like he owns the place, raising an eyebrow at the gun, not pausing for even a second. "So, this is the man who you're trying to get over. No luck so far, looks like."

Liam stands in front of me. It could be a bullet or a freight train—or even just an overly controlling record label rep. Whatever comes to hurt me, he'll stand in its path.

The cameraman walks in behind Harry.

I scramble away from the chair and make sure my dress covers everything. My cheeks burn hot. It must be obvious what we're doing in here. The room smells like sex. How much did they catch on camera?

"Give me that," Liam says, soft and dangerous.

Harry gives an insouciant half smile. "So you can watch it later?"

The cameraman looks alarmed, but he doesn't immediately leave the room. Which means he doesn't understand how serious Liam is. I think Harry understands. He just doesn't care.

The air fills with deadly intent. It doesn't matter that I'm not scared of Liam. He wouldn't hurt me, but the same isn't true for a stranger. Especially one who's trying to check me out while a gun is pointed at his face. "Do you have a death wish?" I snap. "Get out of here."

He grins. "It's boring upstairs. Turns out the party's down here."

Liam holsters his weapon, but he doesn't relax his stance. If anything he looks coiled, ready to leap. It's a different kind of danger, the threat of his fists as he faces off. "Samantha didn't consent to that video. You're going to take out the memory card and hand it over."

"She signed a contract," the cameraman says, sounding flustered.

"It's okay," I say, trying to sound confident. He doesn't have any right to act possessive, not when he keeps warning me away. *What will keep you safe now?* I will. "We can talk to the record label tomorrow and make sure it's not going to make it to production."

There is a moment of stillness. Then Liam moves like a predator, snatching the camera from the other man's arms. Slamming it to the ground. A crunch of metal and plastic and glass. The camera lies in broken pieces on the floor.

The cameraman looks shocked. Harry seems amused.

I stare at the camera in horror. "Why did you do that? Do you know how much that cost? I have no idea, but probably a lot. I have to work with these people, Liam."

"They don't need to know how you sound when you come."

My cheeks burn. I know Liam only wanted to protect me, but I'd like to learn how to protect myself. "I'm going back to the hotel with Harry."

The hotel. Is Liam staying there? That seems like something he would do. Is he on the same floor? I force myself to push away the curiosity. It doesn't matter.

Liam gives me a warning look. "Be home by midnight."

A curfew. It's almost ironic enough that I could laugh. Home? I have a nice suite of rooms at L'Etoile, but it isn't home. Even so, I know I'll obey the order. So much has changed. There are some things that stayed the same.

Liam leaves the room in a brush of warm male air.

Harry raises an eyebrow. "You don't know about hate sex, but you're fucking that caveman?"

"I don't hate him. He doesn't hate me."

"Maybe, but it sure as hell didn't look like love."

Didn't it? The question nips at my skin, leaving red marks. There is so much between Liam and me—obligation and desire, power and respect. I love him the way you love the ground you walk on or the air you breathe, with a kind of unquestioning acceptance. I think maybe he loves me, too, the way the air can fill the lungs and then blow away. He wants to be part of me. As long as he can leave.

CHAPTER SEVEN

Composer Elgar wrote the main theme for his cello concerto on a napkin after waking up from dental surgery.

LIAM

I FIND MY brother in the back alley, leaning against the grimy brick wall, smoking a cigarette. He looks lazy and disreputable. No one would guess that he's counted every head inside the Den, that he could kill any one of them before they blinked.

Tension runs through my limbs, thinking of Samantha downstairs with that handsome Harry March fucker. I want to punch the celebrity tenor, but I settle for my brother, my own flesh and blood, throwing a right hook that lands him sprawling in a dank puddle. It startles a cat from behind a trash can, who disappears in a flash of green eyes and shadow fur.

Josh cocks his head, testing whether his jaw is still hinged. It is.

"Fuck," he says, but there's no heat in the

word. He knows he deserves it. Probably his ears are ringing. He picks himself up off the ground with undue care.

He pulls out a box and offers me a cigarette. After a brief pause, I take one. We both light up. I hate the taste of tobacco. I hate what it does to my lungs, but tonight I breathe in deep. Let it speed me up and slow me down. Let it fill me with blackness.

"You couldn't have given me any fucking warning?"

He shrugs in the darkness. "I knew you'd cover me."

Cover him? I did a hell of a lot more than cover him on that leather armchair. I touched heaven, and when I bring the cigarette to my lips, I can still smell her pussy on my fingers.

The metal door rips open. An explosion of light and sound. A laughing woman stumbles into the alley, followed by a man in a rumpled suit. They take one look at me, and their smiles fade. They hurry past us, both of them keeping their heads down.

Josh gives me a sideways glance. "You shouldn't be in the city."

"He's already here. You think I'm going to let her be bait?"

He sighs. "Always with the hero complex."

That makes me snort. All three of the North brothers enlisted as soon as we turned eighteen. I was pulled into special ops for my cold, calculating mind and my sharpshooting. The poison—that, I learned on the job. There are only two reasons the government needs to hide what a soldier does. One, because he's going to kill someone. Or two, because he's going to gather secret information. A spy, basically. That's what they recruited Josh for. He's a fucking chameleon when he wants to be.

"You heard from Elijah?"

Our youngest brother. "Regular updates. Everything's running smoothly."

"Maybe we should just leave the company to him. That would teach him to be a fucking Boy Scout."

Elijah's smarter than both of us, stronger than both of us.

Unfortunately for the United States government, he's also real fucking ethical. That means none of this lying and killing shit would have worked for him. He's got a noble streak a mile wide. Who knows where he got it from?

Childhood in the North family meant chaos and bloodshed. That was on a good day. That was on a normal day, when we could fight over the single box of mac and cheese in the pantry. When we could bet on a fight between wild dogs in the yard because it distracted us from the hell that was our life.

When it got quiet, that's when you had to worry. Even the feral animals knew to stay away then.

I drop the cigarette to the ground and put it out with my boot. "Speaking of standing out, it's really fucking obvious what your problem is."

"A problem with authority figures, reactionary, a deep vein of self-interest."

"I told you to stop reading your psych evals."

"Then what's my problem?" His tone is taunting, because he really does have a problem with authority figures. Except the chameleon has finally found something he can't hide.

"The way you keep staring at the pretty dancer."

"She's a gymnast," he says, his voice sharp.

"This gonna be a problem?"

He makes a rough sound, like he's insulted. I don't question his ability to do his job. Then again I've never seen him be interested in a woman beyond a ten-minute flirtation and a quick fuck. "It's not going to be a problem."

"You sure?"

He leans his head back and laughs, smoke pluming in the night air. "Don't worry. There's a reason you gave this gig to me and not Elijah. If I see her dear old daddy, I'm going to shoot first and ask questions later. You aren't the only one who can kill without a conscience."

"Good."

"So he wants to use her as bait. Did it ever occur to you to let him have her? Your whole fucking life for the past six years has been about making up for that night. Maybe it's time she just fucking died already. Then you could finally be free."

Before I can even think, I have my arm across his throat, pressing hard enough so he can't breathe. His eyes glitter in the dark. He doesn't even fight me, the bastard. "Don't fucking say that," I say, pulling back with a snarl. Now that I see the smirk on his face, I realize he was baiting me. It worked.

"This is why they get to use her as bait. Because you lose your fucking head wherever she's concerned. She's the weakest part of you, laid out on a platter for your enemies."

"She's the strongest part of me." I would still be a mindless killing machine if I'd never found her, drowning in bodies and blood. She made me breathe again.

My brother is right about one thing. If I wasn't so fucking gone for her, her father couldn't use her as bait. I put her in danger just by caring about her.

SAMANTHA

THERE IS NO reason for me to go looking for Liam. He made me come. My panties are damp because he touched me and touched me. But I don't owe him anything. He didn't act like I did, except I saw the bulge in his black cargo pants. I felt the tension in his body.

It isn't really for sex, the way I scan the dance floor looking for him.

Make yourself feel good. This is all you have. All you'll have if you chain yourself to me. Not a stage. Not a goddamn future.

Is that really how he sees himself? No wonder he doesn't let himself be with me. What would it be like to go through life believing you would ruin the people you love?

There's no sign of him. Disappointment sinks in my stomach.

The woman with blonde curls still sits on the

last stool, though the crowd around her has thinned. I remember what Bethany told me about her. *That's Penny. She runs this place, along with her husband, Damon Scott.* She cocks her head at me, as if I'm some equation she can solve. Then she hops off the stool and crosses the room. I glance behind me, as if expecting her to come for someone else.

"Big muscles, scary scowl?" she says by way of introduction.

That would describe Liam North. "Do you know him?"

"He went that way." She points toward a back exit, and I follow her directions with a wave of thanks. It's only as I push open the door to a black night that I wonder whether it's really safe out here. Two men lean against the wall. The moonlight barely shows me their faces, but I recognize the profiles even in the dark. They turn to face me.

"Make sure no one bothers us."

Josh snorts. "Yeah, I'll be your human sock on the doorknob. I'll make sure no one interrupts you, big brother. Have fun, kids."

My cheeks burn at the implication. Then I'm left alone with Liam. We aren't going to do anything in this alleyway, are we? *I'll be your human sock on the doorknob.* I may not have gone to college, but I know what that means. It means sex.

"Why do you think I wouldn't have a future if you were with me?"

He doesn't seem surprised that I asked. "Because that's what I do to people. That's the effect I have. That's all I can offer you."

"What about the people who work for you? You give them more than a job. You give them a sense of belonging when they didn't think they'd find that again. You give them loyalty and security and a way to live again."

"You make me sound like goddamn Mother Teresa."

"I see the good in you, Liam. And that's only what you do for other people. What you do for me? I *only* have a future because of you. I know I don't say thank you enough—"

A growl cuts me off. "You better not be thanking me for feeding you and giving you clothes, like you're fucking Oliver Twist asking for more gruel."

"Your cooking tastes a lot better than gruel."

"Barely."

"And of course you did more for me than food and clothes. You cared about me. And I'm so grateful that you—"

He cuts me off with his mouth over mine, a twisted punishment for gratitude he does not want, a possession that shows exactly how much he does care about me. Beyond food and clothes. Beyond that of a guardian for his ward. His tongue slides against mine in a sensual caress, and the place between my legs turns liquid, ready for him to touch me again.

He drops a hand to cover my breast, his thumb sweeping over the tip. It's masterful the way he touches me. And lonely, to be the only one who climaxes. I don't want that to happen again. I don't want to be bent over the chair, having an orgasm while he watches. While he wants and wants. I know it gives him pleasure to see me come, but don't I deserve that, too?

I step back and place my hand on his chest. A warning. A command. Maybe I'm inspired by watching the woman on the stool in the Den. The feminine power of her. I want that for myself. "It's my turn to touch you. To taste you."

"No. Not here."

"Where then?" I ask, my voice a challenge. "In a house with a white picket fence? With a balcony and flowers growing up the sides?"

It's a domestic bliss he and I will never know,

not after I lived as his ward in his sterile military compound. There's only this dark alley and the moments we steal. I drop to kneel, looking up at him, daring him to push me away.

"You deserve better," he says, his voice as rough as the gravel under my knees.

"No," I say, reaching for the placket of his pants. "This is exactly what I deserve."

He falls heavy onto my palm, already throbbing as if he's this close to coming, already wet at the tip when I touch there with my forefinger. He makes a sound like he's dying. "I'm close," he mutters. "Just stroke me. Use your fist. Make me come."

So I won't have to kiss him, lick him. So I won't have to dirty myself that way. Except this man isn't dirty. I'm going to make him believe that. So I press a kiss to the crown of his cock. He gasps out my name. "*Samantha.*"

I want him to feel as much pleasure as he gave me.

And I want him to feel as helpless as I did, bent over that chair.

The ridge of his cock feels hard beneath my tongue. I swirl around it, breathing in through my nose, scenting his musk. A spurt of salt hits my tongue, and he grunts. He's on a razor's edge, and

I try to keep him there. Even if it hurts. Even if I'm cruel. I suck gently, not giving him enough pressure to finish, not using my fist the way he wanted. My fingers are gentle over the foreign landscape of his cock. The vein on the underside. The velvet-iron skin. The tight knot of his balls underneath. His heavy pants bounce off the bricks.

"Please," he says, a man facing the end. "Let me fuck you."

That's how I relinquish my hold on his cock. I let him grasp my hair, gentle at first, almost petting me. Then harder, clenching the strands in his fist, tugging at my scalp. He holds me still as his hips take over the rhythm. He fucks me without mercy, without any deference to my inexperience or the fact that I can't breathe. My eyes water, and I know he's finally taking me like he wants. For once, *for once,* he's not holding back. When he comes, his roar fills my ears. His come warms my mouth. He shudders against me, made powerful and brought low by the touch of my lips.

I'm back at the hotel at 11:30 p.m. Only as I take the elevator up to my room do I remember the question I asked Liam—and that he never answered. How did he know my dad threatened to sell the violin? He said they'd never even spoken. And I never told him. It's a small thing. Inconsequential. The fact is that my dad *didn't* sell the violin. It wasn't a problem. I fall asleep with the question hovering at the edge of my brain. How did he know?

CHAPTER EIGHT

In order to ensure perfectly fitted costumes, Cirque du Soleil does a 3D scan of every performer's body. That way, each costume requires few adjustments.

SAMANTHA

MUSIC IS THOUGHT to be an academic pursuit. A cerebral one. The truth is that our bodies are our instrument. We have to train our muscles and build endurance the same way a professional athlete does. I can play for hours, but standing here with my arms raised, being poked and prodded by a seamstress? I'm exhausted. Every muscle screams, but I hold my pose. Piles of ruffles form the blue satin skirt. White lace wraps around my torso. It's a complement of sexy and innocent, and I have to admit it's masterfully done, even if the elderly Russian woman sewing it onto my body is a sadist. A needle pricks my side, and I yelp. The dressmaker holds up a length of cloud-white lace smeared red with blood, her string of Russian accusing. I press my lips together to keep from saying anything. If she were more careful, I wouldn't have bled on the fabric. She's already back at work, sewing and measuring and working, treating me like I'm a mannequin who doesn't need to pee.

Harry March swings from the ropes above us, dangling his feet twenty feet above the stage. "Naughty soloist. Always bleeding when she's pricked."

I stick my tongue out at him, but the effect is ruined when he leers at me. His purple tux arrived earlier today, fitting perfectly to his lean body, created by the third-generation Italian tailor he uses. Because apparently that's how he gets his clothes.

A whirlwind of sound filters from backstage.

"Ah, the fine Mr. Ocha," Harry says, spinning down in a graceful flurry of purple coattails. "The famed composer of the Tanglewood orchestra."

Oh shit. I crane my neck to see a wizened Japanese man with a white goatee and spectacles so shiny they look like mirrors. Another prick of the pin, and this time I glare at the costumer. That was on purpose. It's embarrassing to be caught in the midst of costuming for this meeting. We're both professional musicians. I should be serious and respectful. Instead I'm forced to stand still for him to walk around. My hands clench and unclench uselessly at my sides. "I'm so sorry," I say, face flaming. "Mr. Ocha. It's truly an honor."

He gives a formal bow. "Do not worry yourself, Ms. Brooks. I gave you no notice."

Harry ducks under my arm and extends his hand. "Harry March, at your service. I understand it's quite an honor to play for a man with my talent and renown, et cetera, et cetera. I'm sure you'll do fine."

Mr. Ocha gives a soft laugh. "If you think to put me off with your diva attitude, trust that I have worked with some of the most mercurial temperaments in my career."

"Then you'll be old hat at dealing with Samantha here."

"No, no, he's kidding around. I promise." The words ring hollow as I'm standing on a pedestal, surrounded by yards of imported fabric.

The conductor cocks his head, the mirrored spectacles making him seem unblinking. "No, I don't think you're a diva. Though I've seen you play. It would be warranted if you were."

That gives me pause. "You've seen me play?"

"In London."

That was when I met Beatrix. When we both played for the Queen herself. I had been so excited and so terrified. So determined to make my father proud. Of course he hadn't cared. He only cared about the hands he could shake and the people he could meet.

The conductor is still talking about my performance, the words raining down around me. "You were a revelation, of course. A... how do you say? Anomaly."

That makes Harry laugh, revealing white teeth. "That's Samantha. Very strange."

"It is strange," Mr. Ocha says, his voice heavy. "For a person to be so wholly made of music. I have an orchestra full of musicians. Very talented people. They care deeply about the song and the show. And when they go home at the end of the day—they have, what? Families. And hobbies. They have a life outside of the instrument. People like Samantha, they were made for one thing."

A rock sinks in my gut. What if he's right? I've blamed Liam North for keeping that distance between us, but what if it's been my fault all along? If it's a choice between the violin and a regular life, I already know which one I'd have to choose.

Which means Mr. Ocha sees more than I want him to.

That's probably what makes him a great conductor. It might be confusing to the audience, seeing someone wave a stick back and forth and then gather all the praise. The work happens before the performance, finding strengths and melding styles, turning one hundred strains into a single song.

I swallow past the lump in my throat. "You say that as if it's a foregone conclusion, Mr. Ocha. Doesn't choice factor into the equation?"

The violin means everything to me, but for much of my life, it was all I had. The only comfort I was offered. The only solace. Does the past bind me? Did I learn only to feel through the bow and the strings? Are love and domesticity something forever out of my reach?

He pulls his glasses off his nose, revealing rheumy eyes almost as opaque. *Blind. He's blind.* Somehow I had read everything there was to know about the Tanglewood Orchestra and not found that detail. It made me wonder what else was left out of the official references.

He works a handkerchief over the lenses. "Choice? It has not been my experience that it matters much, Ms. Brooks. Can a violin choose to be a piano? We are what we are."

SAMANTHA

THERE HAVE ALWAYS been songs in my head. Fast and slow. Playful and sad. I didn't think they were unusual. Doesn't everyone hear the music? I also didn't assume I had to write them down. They could only be for me. Ironically it was my father who first made me write them down. It was an old-school style of teaching, copying down lines like in a Victorian school. He would show me sheet music, and I would have to write it down the next day, the next week, the next month. The opening stanza became emblazoned in my mind. I started coming up with my own middles and endings, which he didn't appreciate. He wanted a rote recitation. Two times two equals four. Three times three equals nine. I wanted musical calculus. I wanted it to approach infinity but never quite reach.

I'm sitting in the sound room where we're going to record the album. The songs will premiere on NPR and classical music podcasts. Signed CDs will be on sale at the concerts. The album and the concert tour complement each other, boosting each other, creating a wave within the fandom. It's taken a week of recording to get the pieces together. Now I'm more comfortable facing a large black circle as my audience. On the coffee break, I touch off the opening stanza from my childhood. There are some things you don't think to question as a little girl. Your father tells you to memorize pages of music, you do it. Now I wonder where he even found it. It's not particularly pretty. I suppose that was part of the appeal for him. There's almost a military beat. When I add my own composition, the melody in my head, that's when it departs. I still like the beginning, though. Maybe it provides a contrast. Childhood to adulthood. Cold, ruthless counting to a song from my creative springs.

I finish with a small flourish, then squeak as I see Dierdre standing in the doorway. She holds two lattes, one apparently for me. I take it from her with a murmured thanks.

"Did you write that?" she asks, her tone impassive. I can't tell whether she thinks it's terrible or passably good, but I'm not going to lie when I've been caught.

"Yes."

She falls gracefully onto one of the plastic seats forming a circle. "It's emotive. Heartrending. Mysterious. Like there's something happening beneath the surface."

My pulse thrums with irrepressible pride. The only person who's ever heard my composition before is Liam, and let's face it, he's going to be biased. "You think so?"

"I'm not blowing smoke up your ass. Honestly, I thought you were kind of lame before, but now I see you were just hiding. You're actually super talented."

That startles a laugh from me. "Thanks, I guess."

"I know the way you play is incredible, but there's a difference between technical playing and feeling the music. Sometimes you're a little robot-y."

"Robot-y?" The very weird thing is that I've had that thought about her. Her voice is clear and high and utterly without emotion. Is it just that we can't recognize the emotion in the other's art? Or are we sensitive to the flaws we share?

"I'm sure you don't mean it that way."

She's hit upon my deepest fear, and even knowing she likes my composition, I can't help the shifting sands from sinking me. "Right. Well. Thanks for the coffee."

That doesn't seem to be the end of the conversation. She glances at my open violin case, where a couple of secondhand books I picked up at the Friends of Tanglewood Library book sale rest. An annotated version of Through the

Looking Glass, with notes about symbolism and allegories. "It's possible the Queen of Hearts is based on Queen Victoria," I offer, because that's the part she plays, though she doesn't cut anyone's head off in the show.

She pushes the worn hardcover aside, finding a biography of Lewis Carroll underneath. "Do you believe what they say about him?"

Knots form in my stomach. "To be honest, I didn't know about it. I got those books a week ago, and I've been reading them. It's…definitely unsettling."

That had been an unwelcome discovery, that Lewis Carroll had relationships with many young girls. Were they inappropriate? No one really knows. There's no definitive proof, but our modern lens has learned to be wary of men with power they could abuse. I felt sick when I read about some of his friendships, the contents of his letters.

The nude photographs he took of young girls.

Her eyes turn dark. She looks as if she's seen everything in the world. As if she's judged the universe and found it wanting. It makes me wonder what happened to her. "Would you have suggested Alice in Wonderland as the theme if you had read the biography before?"

"I don't know. Probably not." I look away, trying to remember the way the rest of the music went that my father made me memorize. The only part I kept was the beginning. "Do you think you can separate the writer from his books?"

"Not any more than you can be separated from your music."

"That's what I thought." The opening stanza of my composition is the prime example. It's a remnant of my childhood. A representation of what I lost. A transition to what I've become. You can't wish that away, even if the past is unsavory.

Her blue gaze meets mine. "The relationship with Lewis Carroll and Alice Liddell. It's not something you've experienced, have you?"

My breath catches. She's asking if there's been someone inappropriate with me. I suppose the answer is yes in the strictest sense. Liam's relationship with me isn't like a father. It isn't quite a friend. A protector. A lover. The sun and the moon.

I don't think Dierdre would understand, but that's okay. Sometimes the music isn't for other people. Sometimes it's only meant to be played in private. "Have you?" I ask.

A faint smile. "Yes."

"I'm sorry," I say, meaning it.

"You should play your song onstage," she says. "Fuck the label."

"Maybe." I pick up my bow to begin practicing the Glass Concerto again. Dierdre is more of a tragic figure than I realized. She has darkness in her past that makes me ache, but I don't appreciate her insulting my playing with a blithe *no offense!* Of course it's offensive. She knows that. "Maybe not. I'm not a robot when I play someone else's music. I'm sorry that you don't like it, but there are people who do. And I'm one of them."

LIAM

WHEN THE RECORD label reps leave, I allow myself to slip into the sound room. The engineer nods to me. We've already spoken. A large window divides the two rooms. Samantha's absorbed in a conversation with the conductor, so she doesn't notice me right away. A faint flush pinkens her cheeks. Her eyes sparkle with excitement that only comes from a great session. If we were at home, it would take her hours to wind down before she'd be calm enough for sleep. Of course, we aren't at home. We never will be, certainly not as guardian and ward.

Mr. Ocha gives her a small but meaningful

bow before he leaves the room. She will have to work with a new conductor in every city. More than any of the other performers, her work will be entwined with each orchestra. It will be a challenge for any violinist—one I'm confident she will handle with grace and quiet command. Conductors like this one will appreciate her talent. A more ego-filled conductor will face her steel core.

Her brown eyes meet mine, and my breath catches. If she were only a little less beautiful, maybe I could have helped falling for her. Maybe I wouldn't want to bend her over the music stand and ride her from behind, testing the world-class acoustics in the small room a different way.

I head into the room, keeping my distance. Because she *is* that beautiful. It would be enough to stop any man, to make him stare and want and harden. Even before he knew about her breathtaking talent.

"Did you hear me play?" she asks, sounding excited. There's no doubt that she was incredible. Not even in her own mind. That's what it means to have the kind of skill she does.

"I'm going to."

Now she looks bashful. "You want me to play for you?"

For me and no one else, because my baser impulses know no boundaries. Luckily there's enough of the man inside me to know she needs this. She deserves it. "I want you to play your music."

Her eyes widen. She knows what I mean. Her composition. The music she wrote. It's been in my head since I caught her playing it. When she walked out of my house, her music stayed behind.

It's the backdrop of my dreams.

"It's not in the album."

I make a noncommittal sound. It's not in the album because Samantha hasn't played it for them. She knows her power as a soloist, but not as a composer. "That doesn't matter. We have the room for the next hour. Play it. Record it. Produce it. A label will distribute it if this one doesn't. Or put it up on YouTube yourself. Or just give me a CD for my birthday, if nothing else."

That makes her smile, like I hoped it would. "Who said you were getting a birthday present this year?"

"You don't have to do anything with it, but we have the hour in the studio." I glance through the window at the sound engineer, who gives us a thumbs-up. It costs a hefty sum to rent the space and equipment. It's not even a fraction of what she's worth.

Her hand tightens on her violin. She wants to do it. She's afraid. Which means I already know the choice she's going to make. This was not a little girl who let fear stop her. As a woman, she's unbreakable.

"Will you stay here?"

I have to clear my throat before I can speak. "It would be my honor."

The first touch of her bow changes the air in the room. The light. It's more than sound she makes with that violin. It's feeling and motion. It's energy. The melody runs through my veins, stirring long-dormant memories. The notes are high and haunting. There's a small knit of skin between her eyebrows. Does the music help her remember? Or does it help her forget?

The music makes me think about hope, which is something I try to avoid. Samantha was twelve years old when I got custody of her. When I was twelve there was a teacher who understood what was happening at home. Well, most teachers understood on some level. They looked the other way. They tried not to think about my protruding ribs and bruises.

This teacher tried to help. She insisted on it,

bringing a sack lunch for me every day. I suppose I was as simple as a stray dog back then. Feed me and I start to trust, even though I know I shouldn't. She slipped money into my backpack. Small amounts. A few dollars here. Enough to get food for Josh and Elijah at home. It was enough to make me think things could get better.

So when she asked me to tell the principal what was happening, I did. The police came and took the three of us away. We packed our worn, ill-fitting clothes into plastic grocery bags. An elderly couple looked at us the way they might a pack of rabies-infested dogs, when we were dropped off on their doorstep. For three nights we slept with our bellies full.

That's what the music makes me remember.

The way the court ordered us back into my father's custody. He knew better than to punish me by then. I had learned to be numb. Instead he put Josh and Elijah into the well and doused the rope in gasoline. It burned in my hands as I tried desperately to put it out. Then my father locked the door to the house, leaving me to sit outside the well, helpless and eaten through with guilt.

This is what hope brought us. Josh's arms shaking with the effort of holding the toddler up in the water. Elijah drinking the water and then vomiting it back up. Twelve hours was a lifetime.

I never tried to help them again. Never let myself hope again. Never let myself feel until Samantha walked into my life, somehow unbroken by the wasteland of her own childhood.

CHAPTER NINE

Before the performance of Charles Gounod's Faust, only thirty pounds of tickets had been sold. The organizer gave away tickets for the first three nights and then advertised the show as being "sold out." Paying customers could only attend the fourth night. By popular demand, the show was extended past the advertised run.

SAMANTHA

"WHAT DO YOU love most about Harry March?"

I can feel my face freeze into an uncomfortable smile. It's been easy enough to ignore the cameras on the side of the stage. They're pretty unobtrusive, enough that it makes me wonder how they're going to make an interesting behind-the-scenes show out of this.

"His voice is incredible," I say, meaning it. He strolls across the stage during rehearsals, sometimes without a mic, and his voice carries throughout the whole theater. When he really pours his heart into the music, which isn't often, the hair on the back of my neck rises. "He's really a musical genius. The way he approaches pitch, there's this subtle interplay of—"

The host laughs. Ricky Lightfoot is the voice of multiple reality TV shows, including Real Estate in Rio and Fighting Chefs. The way he gives commentary in each episode makes it feel like he's part of the action, though he's never actually onscreen except in the interviews—and now I realize that's really his only connection to the characters. Of course, now I'm one of the characters. The fictionally real version of me.

I watched a few online last night to prepare for the interview. Bethany and Romeo went before us. Dierdre waits on the sidelines for her turn.

"Of course he's a fabulous singer," Ricky says, reminding me of the reporter from Classical Notes last year. "I mean on a personal level. I understand you've been spending a lot of time together preparing for the album and the tour."

I glance at Harry, who only wears a secret smile. It seems to confirm that something *is* going on between us. He reclines on the loveseat, his arm thrown across the back. It had seemed cozy when we first sat down. Maybe something to make us fit in the camera angle better. Now it feels pointed.

"All the performers are great," I say cautiously. "Everyone's been really kind and professional."

"Professional." There's a smirk on Ricky's orange-tan face.

A nervous laugh escapes me. "This is my first time really touring, and I want it to go well. So I'm working really hard and focusing on the music."

"Let's take a look at some clips."

Dramatic music plays. Colors flash across a big screen behind us. There's footage of Harry and me at the first dinner, giving glances at each other across the table. I swear in one of them I was looking at someone's dessert, giving it these crazy hungry eyes, but it looks like I'm doing that to Harry. And he's doing it right back, sliding glances to me and then away.

A cut scene with more dramatic music, and then Harry and I are onstage. I remember that day. The label reps were trying to get us to dance this spinning ballet move, which I absolutely cannot do. I'm falling, and he's catching me, both of us laughing. We look like two lovers being playful, not two musicians being asked to dance and doing it horribly.

I glance at Harry and find that he's watching me. My expression turns questioning. Did he know they were going to spin it like this? Does he mind? I remember his warning from that dinner. *Those record label people aren't here to keep us together. They're here to tear us apart. This tour is going to be headline news one way or another.*

I'm not a gorgeous starlet who walks the red carpet. Having a relationship with me doesn't seem like headline news, but maybe they're desperate. Unease turns my stomach.

Another round of dramatic music and a flashing montage of notes.

The images turn darker. It looks like some kind of empty building. Or a parking garage? My heart leaps into my throat. It's a back alley. The back alley behind the Den. A man and woman press against the wall. They're only shadows right now. You can't tell who they are, but I already know. Spots dance in front of my eyes. Adrenaline tastes metallic on my tongue. Someone was videotaping us? I thought Liam destroyed the camera in the music room. I thought Josh made sure we weren't watched. Apparently not. *They're here to tear us apart.*

The couple turns so the man leans against the wall, completely melded into the night. It's the woman who takes a step back, her hand still reached out to his chest. The headlight of a passing car flashes into the space. Her black dress and dark curls could belong to anyone, but for a split second, her features are unmistakable. It's me. Bile rises in my throat that someone saw us. That *everyone* is going to see this.

She gets down on her knees, this woman in shadows again, anonymous in the dark, and yet *not* anonymous because the viewer has already seen her. The video fades into blackness, but it's blatantly clear what happens next in the story.

Harry studies me with a cool detachment. It takes me a minute to understand the fake story they've built. The man was mostly in shadow. Liam was mostly in shadow. People will believe that it was Harry who was in that alley with me. "Why are you doing this?"

That now-familiar nonchalant smile. "I'm not doing anything, sweetheart."

"You are," I say through clenched teeth, not caring that they're still recording the interview. It doesn't really matter. Clearly they can make the tape show anything they want. "Bethany told me you asked for me on this tour. Demanded me. Why?"

"Maybe I liked you," he says with a wink. "I liked you in the alleyway very much."

"That wasn't you!"

He gives a shrug. "Wasn't it? We aren't going to comment, naturally."

Indignation makes my cheeks hot. "We aren't going to comment on anything because this video isn't going to air." I glare at the host. "I'm serious about this."

"It's not network television," he says as if by way of explanation. "The streaming distributors can get away with almost anything. And you weren't even naked."

"I don't care what's allowed. This isn't happening."

Ricky looks sympathetic. "Are you worried what Harry's ex-girlfriend is going to think when she sees this? They've only been broken up for—what? Six months?"

All those hours of practice. Years of it, when you add up the time. All that worry about music and artistry and professionalism, and this is what people care about. My jaw clenches. "You're a fraud, you know that? You know that isn't him, and you don't even care."

He doesn't look bothered by my comment. I imagine he's heard worse. "I'm a journalist by training, but that's not what I do now. No, I'm an entertainer. And the story of your relationship with Harry March is far more entertaining than the fact that you blew some random guy at a club."

A trickle of relief filters through my frustration. At least they don't know the man in the alley was Liam North. I imagine it would be *entertaining* to Ricky to talk about my sexual relationship with my former guardian on the streaming distributor.

"I'm not going to be a part of this," I say, standing to leave.

Harry gets up with me. "For what it's worth, every man watching will wish they were in that alley."

Ricky stands, as casually as if we'd ended the interview on great terms. "Though if I were to put on my journalist hat, I would have to ask you where exactly Harry's girlfriend is right now."

Harry's tension fills the air. "She has a right to privacy."

"Indeed. One of the benefits of fame and large sums of money. Then again, what would it look like if she simply disappeared? Who would know? How long would it take to come out?" Ricky looks thoughtful, but it's all a pretense. He's probing. This is what a real interview with him would be like, and I realize that the playboy chatting about home renovations and tomato sriracha foam is just an act. "And I suppose, more importantly, who would be responsible for something like that?"

"We're leaving," Harry says, his jaw tight. He steers my elbow toward the door, and even though I'm pissed at him, I want to leave badly enough that I let him escort me out.

SAMANTHA

I HAVE AN agent who works out of LA. She represents a lot of famous classical musicians. I'm small potatoes compared to most of the names on her client list. I think the only reason she ended up representing me is that Liam North doesn't accept anything but the best for me. She's always been kind on the phone, but we've never been chatty.

Which is why it's super awkward to call her to talk about a blowjob.

"Samantha," she says, her gravelly voice warm. I imagine her as someone with bouffant hair who smokes two packs a day, though her barebones website didn't have a photo. She's one of those old-school people who makes deals by phone and fax. "How's the tour going?"

"Good. Great! Okay, not the best."

A low laugh. "Tell me the problem, and I'll see what I can do."

She worked on the contract with the label, mostly to make sure I didn't sign myself into indentured servitude. We didn't really discuss all the terms. I could never have imagined this particular problem anyway. "So the label is doing this reality show special about the tour. I did the interview yesterday, and they have some footage that's... delicate in nature."

"Spell it out for me, honey."

"Well, they're trying to make it look like I'm in a relationship with Harry March. I guess it's a publicity thing? That part is weird enough, except they also caught me in a compromising position. With someone else."

She sucks in a breath. "How compromising?"

I remember the taste of salt on my tongue. The clench of Liam's hands in my hair. "Very."

"You may not want to hear this, but that's actually a good thing. If it were tame, they could argue it was fair game. There's a modesty clause in your contract. They can't stick a camera in your dressing room and sell photos of you."

My stomach turns. "People do that?"

"I've been in this business long enough to see everything. Classical music is its own beast. I've got these actresses wishing their sex tapes would go viral, but in the music world, half the conductors won't work with someone if their skirt is too short."

"The thing is, I wasn't exactly naked. And neither was the… other party. But we were clearly, you know." If my cheeks get one degree hotter this hotel suite is going up in flames. File this under conversations I thought I'd never ever have.

"The modesty clause will cover it."

"So you can fix it?" I ask hopefully.

"I can fix it. Make sure there are no cameras around next time you don't get exactly naked. I can keep the record label in line, but not the paparazzi."

I hang up with the word *paparazzi* ringing in my head.

It was one thing to go on tour as the sideshow, the small player in a big production. Why would the paparazzi even care about me? It feels like I'm living someone else's life. It's happening so fast. When I was under Liam's roof, all I wanted was to grow up. To be independent. To live this life of performance and music.

I can admit now that I didn't fully understand what it entailed. I probably couldn't have understood it without living it. And I can appreciate why Liam wanted me to have a normal high school upbringing before this.

A sound comes from the sitting area. I leave the room and run directly into Josh, who does not appear at all ashamed of having listened to my conversation. He raises an eyebrow. "Not exactly naked? Is that what the kids are calling it these days?"

"God. That was a private conversation."

"What you did in the alley was supposed to be private, and look how that turned out." His voice turns soft and mocking. "You're a famous musician, now. You don't get privacy."

My eyes narrow. "You were supposed to make sure we were alone."

"Ah, yes. It's possible there was a black Suburban across the street with a lens poking out the window. I couldn't be sure without crossing the street, and I'm extremely lazy."

Shock makes me speechless. "Why?"

"This is your life now, Samantha. Don't string my brother along because he's a good fuck. You want the spotlight? Fine. That's not Liam. He's put his life on hold for six years taking care of you—now you've finally left, and he's still doing it."

"You are *such* an asshole."

"Why don't you go running to Liam and whine about it?" he asks, taunting.

"Because my agent is going to get it removed. No thanks to you."

"Good. Because it's not only your security at stake."

My heart thuds. "What do you mean?"

"Liam being in Tanglewood? It puts him in danger. You should send him away for his own sake. If you actually cared about him, you'd make him leave."

I swallow against the dryness. "Do you think this tour is putting him at risk?"

Josh gives me a dark glare. "You put him at risk."

CHAPTER TEN

Italian composer and string player Claudio Monteverdi once said, "Music is spiritual. The music business is not."

SAMANTHA

"ONE WEEK, PEOPLE. Get it together."

She doesn't mean people. She means me. My arms burn from holding the position. My legs ache. It's actually my ass that hurts the most. Who knew my butt muscles needed to prepare for this tour? We have one week until opening night, and the rehearsal still looks like a middle school theater production. Actually, I think we're regressing. It's getting worse.

Tracy of talent development gives me a brittle smile. "Arabesque is about the extension of your limbs and the space in your chest. You look like you're about to fall over."

"That's because I'm about to fall over." Sweat drips into my eyes, and I let my limbs fall. "This isn't working. I'm not a ballerina. I've never been a ballerina."

"No, no." Staci's voice is soothing. She's the good cop to Tracy's bad cop routine. "This isn't about actual ballet. Our audience is looking for the *appearance* of ballet."

"I don't understand." I hold out my hand, which trembles slightly from this choreography they've had me doing for the past five hours. "And I don't think I can play the violin like this."

Tracy purses her lips. "Am I supposed to tell the record label you're refusing?"

Acid rises in my stomach. I feel like I'm being punked, like someone is going to pop out with video cameras and confetti, everyone laughing, because they made a violinist try to do ballet. Except it isn't actually funny. No one's going to make this stop, so I have to do it. "I guess… yes. I'm sorry but I respectfully refuse to do this pretend ballet."

There's silence in the theater. Bethany and Romeo stand to the side, their skin sheened with sweat—except the difference is they don't do the appearance of gymnastics. They do actual gymnastics. They're athletes. Beatrix isn't here because the baby kept her up all night. Harry reclines in the second row, his feet up on the chairs in front of him.

I thought if I could do enough pretend plies

or fake twirls they would be satisfied, but they kept adding to the routine. I don't know what it would have looked like by the end of the day. Maybe the Nutcracker. "I play the violin. That's what I do. If you want me to play the part of Alice, to walk around looking lost at the big trees or to drink from a teacup, that's one thing. But I'm not going to dance."

"Fucking finally," Harry shouts from the seats.

He grins at me, his teeth a brilliant, manufactured white. No one asked him to do a single plie. No one expected him to give the appearance of ballet. I glare at him from the center of the stage. "What does that mean?"

"It means I've been waiting for you to stand up to them. Honestly, how you can give orders to that Neanderthal at the Den but take orders from these two? No offense."

"How is that *not* offensive?"

He pulls out something that looks suspiciously like a joint and lights up, right there in a theater seat. Ashes could drop onto the red velvet. He raises an eyebrow, as if daring me to reprimand him. "You are missing the point. Our audience doesn't want the appearance of ballet. They want what they fucking came for, which is a fucking show. This is a concert. A rave with a bow tie."

"So I should launch myself into the mosh pit?" I suggest, my tone acerbic. Somewhere along the way I lost my meekness, my natural desire to please. Maybe it was when they made me put on this pale blue leotard that's supposed to approximate Alice's dress.

Harry takes in my body in a slow, obvious way, and I'm reminded what Bethany said about him asking for me to be part of the tour. Demanding it, really. Because he likes the way I look? That feels like a stretch, and I don't only say that because I look skinny and pale in this leotard.

He hadn't even met me before we showed up for the tour.

"It can't hurt," he says about the mosh pit idea. "Well, unless they don't catch you. Then I suppose that will hurt a lot. Still, I expect most of these assholes would rather put their hands on you."

"If you were waiting for me to stand up for myself, why didn't you say something?"

"Where's the fun in that?"

Frustration makes my chest tight. "This is important. This is a big deal. It may not seem like it to you—but to Bethany and Romeo. To Beatrix. To me. This is a once-in-a-lifetime chance."

He does not look impressed. Instead he laughs. "God, you're so fucking naïve."

Hurt burns through my skin, making me lash out. "And you're so fucking… so fucking mean."

It's not exactly the most creative insult, but it seems to do the trick. His insouciant smile disappears. And I realize that I'm standing on a massive stage, shouting at Harry March. Is this my life right now? Maybe I really have stepped through the looking glass, where everything is topsy turvy.

"I'm sorry," I whisper, though no one can hear me. Tears burn my eyes, but I force them back as I flee backstage. My violin case leans against the wall. I didn't even need to pull it out today. They know that I can play the music. The part about acting like Alice—that's a little daunting. I'm not an actress. But I'd give it my best shot. The dancing, though… I drop my head, feeling defeated.

From behind the thick velvet curtains I hear the recorded music start again. They must be running through the steps with Bethany and Romeo. I take out my violin, gently stroking the shiny wood. The violin understands me in a way that no person ever could. *Except for Liam.*

Gently I run my finger across the strings. They vibrate beneath my touch, as if asking to be played. A violin wants to play the way a tree waits for the wind—the only way it can move.

Something catches my eye in the maroon interior of the violin case. A slip of white paper.

I unfold it, my hands still shaking from the exertion of the dance.

Darling. I'm sorry I don't have more time to explain. It will come as a shock, but there's no helping it. You have grown into a beautiful young woman. Stay safe.

It's signed *A. Brooks,* which is the signature my father used. Alistair Brooks.

SAMANTHA

THE ELEVATOR DOORS open to reveal the penthouse, where Hugo stands holding the baby. I've only ever seen Hugo dressed to stylish, masculine perfection. Now he's shirtless, his muscles on full display, a shadow of a beard across his jaw. Loose pants drape low over his hips. He looks rumpled and sexy and extremely domestic. Madeline wears only a cloth diaper, fussing with soft grunts and coos against his shoulder, her little fists tight. "I'm sorry," he says, his voice low. "Bea is still in the shower. She should be out shortly."

"No, don't apologize. I'm the one who barely gave you any notice." I take in the scrunched face of the baby. "Is something wrong? Is she sick? Can I help?"

He clucks in a way that's soothing. "She only wants her *mama* at night, so Beatrix tries to accommodate her. Hours and hours, she does this. I finally made her take a break."

Emotions flood the space between his words—the way my friend would have fought to give everything to her daughter, even at the expense of her own peace. The way Hugo usually caters to Bea in all things, but he felt strongly enough to demand this.

"Let me," I say. They both deserve a break. "Please? She can get to know me."

"She might cry," he warns, but he isn't telling me no.

He turns, and I see the stress in little Madeline's clear blue eyes. She holds an ice pack in her hands, chewing on it with frantic urgency. Hugo murmurs to her in French, and the baby quiets somewhat. Anyone would be soothed. I'm a little soothed, standing near him. It's startling, this affection. My upbringing didn't include hugs or kisses, not with my real father. Not with Liam North. Our relationship had always been about respect and obedience. About protection. It did not include him rubbing my back with his large hand, the way Hugo does now.

"So she will cry, and I'll tell her it will be okay." I sound more confident than I feel. I don't have any experience with babies. I also don't have any experience with domesticity, with fathers who cradle their children the way Hugo does. He hands her to me, so gently, showing me how to support her head.

"Ah," he says, his gravelly voice pleased. "She likes you."

I am no infant whisperer. Madeline does not instantly settle, but she does not seem more worried to be away from her mama and papa. She fidgets against me, as if trying to tell me about her internal angst. "There, there," I whisper, pressing my lips to the impossible softness of her forehead. "You don't have the words yet, but we hear you. We understand, sweet baby."

She grasps the fabric of my dress, holding on. Of course she's always held in arms, always fully supported, but even so it must feel like falling. She can barely hold up her own head. She can't crawl or walk. Always carried. Like Alice tumbling down an endless expanse.

Her scent is uniquely baby, the smell of new-
ness, of hope. I stroke my hand over her smooth
baby-hair, a darker copper than her mother's red
curls.

A sense of overwhelming protectiveness rises
in my chest. Is this how Liam felt? I want to
protect her from everything—a callous world and
shallow boys. From her own emerging teeth. She
sucks hard on the wrapped ice pack, her fists
shaking, but the rest of her slumps against me, as
if grateful for the support.

"Are you sure you're all right?" Hugo asks,
and he gives me this room to demur. The baby is
not bubbly and smiling, so maybe some people
would not want to hold her. I can't imagine
turning a child away for this. She needs us now
more than ever.

"Of course I'm all right. If you need a break,
I'm going to stay right here." I settle onto the
couch to prove my point. Madeline lets out a soft
plaintive sound, and I murmur back to her. It's a
universal language, this. Like music.

He observes me for one more moment before
giving a nod. "Then I'll go check on Bea."

My heart clenches as he goes into the bedroom. What happened before I got here? My

friend is incredibly self-sufficient, but she would also feel guilt that she can't put her child at ease. It must remind her of the times she was without a parent, alone and afraid. Was she crying? I was debating whether or not I should come over tonight, but now I'm so glad I did. Beatrix plays the piano and sings in a soulful voice. I'm not a singer. Not at all, but I still find myself humming a tune before I can stop myself. It could have been anything. Wiegenlied by Brahms. Or Bach's Air on the G string. Instead the notes of my composition fill the air, making my eyes sting with unshed tears. I keep rocking, keep humming, keep holding the warm weight of her, hoping she'll find some comfort in my presence.

She becomes softer in my arms, less clenched. Her little fists open. She grasps a strand of my hair, yanking enough to make me jolt and then laugh softly. "Little troublemaker," I tell her, before the melody takes over again, soothing both of us with its melancholy.

The last note vibrates against my closed lips, and then silence falls.

"That was incredible." Bea leans against the doorframe wearing a ruffled sage green robe, her cheeks pink, her hair a wild mane of darkened, damp curls. "Did you write it?"

My face warms. I never told her I was composing. It was too private. Too terrifying. "Yes."

Her expression only has understanding. She knows how hard it is to put myself out there. "Thank you for taking Madeline. It's been rough at night."

"I wish you told me. I could have been here."

She gives me a dire look. "You're not our babysitter. You should be out there, having fun."

"Bea, I love you like my own sister, but you have a hard time accepting help. Especially when it's not paid. I don't have to be your nanny or your babysitter to want to hold her."

Her face scrunches, making her look adorably like her daughter. "That's not true."

I raise my eyebrows pointedly. "Remember how you met Hugo."

She hired him to take her virginity, even though she's a beautiful young woman—many men would have been happy to divest her of it for free. Her grin is unrepentant. "You may be right."

"So I'll be back tomorrow. And the next night. No arguing."

"I wasn't planning on arguing. Especially when you managed to do *that*."

Madeline's lashes rest against her full cheeks, her lips parted in sleep. The hands that had been in fists are now thrown backward, hanging over my arm in peaceful abandon. "Good."

"Though I probably would have tried to pay you."

I make a face. "I'm not taking your money."

Hugo brings us a tray of tea and pours for us both. Beatrix looks up at him as he hands her a cup; the love and gratitude in her eyes take my breath away. She pauses to grasp his arm, and he looks deeply moved. His throat works in silence. That's the strength of love between them. It's beyond words.

He places a tender kiss to the crown of her head. "I'll leave you alone to speak in private. Only call me if you would like me to take the *bebe.*"

Bea waits until he's gone before turning to me. "Okay, so what were you going to ask me?"

I give her a blank look. "Nothing. I just wanted to see my goddaughter."

"Nice try, but you were really going to ask me something."

Unease moves through me, and Madeline fidgets in her sleep. I take a deep breath until the moment passes. No wonder Beatrix struggles to constantly hold her child—any emotions get passed through, skin to skin. "I was going to ask if you could check the hotel. I wonder if… actually, I think I know that Liam is staying here."

This is where he'd stay if he wanted to watch over me, to be close to me, and I can't fool myself any longer—that's why he's here. He loves me? Yes. Whether it's a parental love or a sexual love or some muddled place in the middle. The knowledge rises inside me, a fountain, spilling over. I don't feel happy. That's too plain a word. There's uncertainty mixed in, dark ink into milky white. He loves me, but he doesn't want to. And he won't be happy that I tracked him down.

Beatrix blinks slowly. "Liam is in Tangle-wood?"

"It's probably too much to hope that he used his real name."

She pulls out her laptop. A few clicks, and a website pulls up with the curling logo for L'Etoile at the top. Alternating grey and white rows show names and room numbers.

There we are, Samantha Brooks and Joshua North on the fifth floor.

She scrolls further down. "I don't see him."

"He might have used a fake name." Disappointment sinks in my stomach. "Though I don't know how I'll find him now. Maybe just hang out at the front desk like a stalker until he shows up."

"I can ask the staff if they know."

The grey-white rows climb the screen. "Wait. Stop. Right there. *F. Kreisler?* That could be Fritz Kreisler. He's my favorite composer. Liam knows that."

"It could be someone's real name. Fiona Kreisler. Faith. Francesca."

The more I stare at the letters, the more I'm sure. "It's him."

"Frederica."

"If it's someone named Frederica Kreisler, I'll offer her turndown service."

"I'm not worried about the hotel. I'm worried about you. Why are you looking for Liam? Why is he even here, under a fake name? Is this about the tour?"

"It's about protection, which is the only way he knows how to love."

"I thought Josh was protecting you."

I bite my lip and look away, pausing for only a second before revealing the truth. "My father is alive. Apparently. I could hardly even believe it when Liam told me except I got this note."

She takes it from me, studying the scrawled words on a scrap of paper. "God, Samantha. I don't even know what to say. This is incredible. Isn't it?"

An old excitement beats against my breast, the kind I felt as a child when my father would come home from work, when he'd take the time to watch me play violin. "Liam doesn't trust him. I guess that makes sense. Why would he have pretended to be dead all this time?"

"He says in the note he can explain." Hope rings in Bea's clear blue eyes. "Imagine. You could be reunited with your father after all this time."

My heart sinks. Of course she would feel only joy at the idea of her father being alive. It's the greatest hope of any orphan, the impossible dream. Perhaps I was cruel to even show this to her, except that she's my friend. For all that our lives have been alike, there are profound differences.

Bea's parents adored her. They left her a fortune, but she would have traded every last cent for another minute in their arms. I don't begrudge her that joy, but it wasn't the same with me. I grieved my father desperately, though it was less about his love for me. He was my only security. The only person to remember that I existed, to pack me in his suitcase and drag me around. Losing him meant losing everything. There was no money, no family, no safety.

A knot forms in my throat. "This is going to

sound crazy, but my loyalty is to Liam now. It has to be. Which means I have to tell him about this."

"You love him." It's not a question. Her eyes well with understanding.

That's the other way our experiences were different. The man who got custody of her—a business partner of her father's—was cold and distant. He left her alone in this penthouse suite. Her anxiety was stronger than any physical lock. He did not need her money, but he liked to control it. He wanted to control *her*.

"I've always loved him." He stood in that Russian orphanage, looking strong and determined. The nuns fussed about paperwork and payments, but he would not relent until I left with him that day. Our lives have never been conventional, but there has always been love. Deep and sure.

CHAPTER ELEVEN

Leoš Janáček composed Intimate Letters inspired by his relationship with a married woman 28 years younger than him. It premiered on September 11, 1928, a month after Janáček died.

SAMANTHA

DENSE CARPETING AND embossed wallpaper swallow my knock. After a minute I'm sure he hasn't heard me. I knock again. Nothing. Does he know I'm here? Is he pissed that I tracked him down?

Of course it might not even be him.

"Mrs. Kreisler?" I say, a half second away from leaving. "Housekeeping."

My spirits fall. I told myself I only wanted to confide in Liam about the note. That I owed him that. It was more, though. I've been starving for the sight of him. Only a few days, a few weeks. A few hours without him, and I start to droop, to wilt, a flower without water.

I turn to leave and run directly into a hard

chest. A shriek escapes me. I only have a second to register the muscles pressed into my face and the familiar warmth before I pull back. "What are you doing?"

He raises an eyebrow. "I was going to ask you the same thing."

Sweat glistens on his neck. A black T-shirt clings to his chest. He isn't breathing hard, but I know from experience that doesn't mean anything. He could have finished a grueling two-hour workout. He probably did. I raise my chin. "I'm looking for you."

Reaching past me, he holds the brass key up to the door. It unlocks with a soft mechanical sound. L'Etoile is an interesting mix of old-world details and modern convenience. "Inside."

Not an invitation. It's an order.

I remain in the hallway. "You used the name Kreisler. Did you know I'd find you?"

He looks like he wants to give more commands. I'm not a man in his regiment. Or a child in his home. The knowledge glints in his eyes. "I hoped so."

I turn my gaze away to hide the flare of hope. It's enough to propel me inside. Frustration forms a knot in my throat. He doesn't think he should touch me, will barely even let himself admit he wants me. That's bad enough, but the way he gives in is almost worse—enough to drive me crazy. Enough to give me hope that we can be together.

The room is more spartan than the suite I have upstairs. More fitting for Liam. A king-size bed with iron scrollwork and an ornate dresser. A flat-screen TV mounted to the wall. A small duffel bag sits in the corner, the only evidence that it's occupied. I have a feeling there are more weapons than clothes in there.

He pulls a bottle of water from the minifridge and downs it in one long swallow. I watch his throat work with reluctant fascination, the pull of masculine tendon and flesh, how he seems both strong and vulnerable at the same time. The empty bottle sails into the trash.

"What happened?"

The question takes me off guard. "How do you know something happened?"

Because he knows me. His gaze challenges me to deny it. He nods toward the gold velvet armchair. It looks completely different from the simple antique dining chair that I used to practice the violin back home, but I feel the same way as I sit down. As if he's measuring me.

"I found this." The note weighs ten thousand

pounds.

He remains standing as he reads, his hard face betraying nothing. When he's finished, he sets it down on the table. So carefully. I know without explanation that he's going to check the paper for prints. I've heard enough murmured conversations about their missions to know the drill. The missions have never been about me before.

"Where was it?"

"My violin case. It was there when I finished rehearsals today."

A vein beats in his neck. That's the only sign that he feels anything. "He got inside the Grand?"

"Don't be mad at Josh. He's doing his best."

He gives me the faintest smile. It's not a soft expression, that smile. Nothing encouraging or sweet. It makes my insides freeze. "Your father got within ten feet of you."

I swallow hard. "You said people might use me against him."

"That could happen."

"Then why is it dangerous for my father to be near me? If he's really alive, I want to see him."

"No."

Frustration rises in my chest. "Don't I get a say in that?"

"No."

"Liam. I'm a grown-up."

"I don't care if you're ninety fucking years old, he's not getting near you."

My eyes narrow. This is always the problem between us. He wants to treat me like a soldier. Someone he can control. The saddest part is that I want his control. I want the safety that comes along with it, but then when would I grow up? "I accepted Josh's protection because of what happened on my eighteenth birthday. That doesn't mean I'm going to do everything you say."

"Jesus Christ. Do you want to be killed?"

It's a knife in the stomach. "This is my father we're talking about."

"And he left you."

The knife twists, plunging deeper. Ripping me open. "Yeah. I got that. You think I don't know? It hurts to think my father died. Somehow it hurts worse to know he was alive and let me get sent to a Russian orphanage. So maybe I want to tell him, did you think of that? To demand answers. Maybe I need to do that for closure."

A growling sound. "You don't need answers."

"I don't think you have any idea what I need, Liam North."

His eyes darken. "I took care of you for six years. You never needed anything."

"Except a hug!"

"What the hell are you talking about?"

"I wanted you to love me. I wanted you to—"

"Look what happened." Rocks scrape across rocks. His voice rumbles over my skin. "When I touched you, look what happened. I kissed you. I fucked you. I took your virginity. Is that what you wanted?"

"*Yes.* And I want you to do it again."

The words hang between us, sharp and jagged. They expose my most tender parts to this man. He looks impassable. Impenetrable. He doesn't crumble. "We'll increase security."

"No. You don't get to make decisions for me. You aren't my father."

He looks pained. "I know that. God, I know that."

"Tell me what's so terrible about my dad that I can't even see him."

He sits down on the edge of the bed, his elbows on his knees, hands pressed together as if he's praying. "You really want to know? Because there's no going back."

Acid laces my throat. "You've been protecting me from it long enough."

A phone appears in my hand. He presses a few things on the screen and hands it to me. There is a picture of my violin, the one I used when I was in Russia. It sits in the case with velvet lining and a hard, plastic exterior. I swipe left. In the next photo the violin is removed. In the next, the velvet is peeled back. There are words written on the underside, symbols I can't decipher. *A code.*

"What is this?" I whisper.

"Your father was a spy for Russia. He filtered information through customs using a few different methods. This was one of them."

My stomach turns over. I always carried the violin with me. No one looked too hard at a shy little girl clutching her instrument. Since it was expensive and on loan, I would carry it with me onto airplanes. It never got checked with the rest of our luggage. "I don't believe you."

"He used you. You were a telephone to him. A bundle of money. A way to smuggle classified documents around in plain sight. That's what you were to him."

"You're wrong."

"Didn't you ever wonder why he let you play the violin, why he paid for lessons when he barely paid for you to have clothes? Why he took breaks from his work for you to attend performances?"

I shook my head, even though I did wonder. They had been the only signs of fatherly love, and

I'd been desperate to interpret them that way. He never seemed very interested in hearing me play. My renown as a child prodigy meant we received invitations regularly to perform in incredible venues—most of which he would refuse. There seemed no rhyme or reason to the ones he accepted.

"Yes," he says, his voice almost tender as it slices me apart. "He would have put you in a freezing cold boarding school in Russia if he didn't need you for this."

A single tear slides down my cheek. "Why are you saying this to me?"

"Because this is the man you want to meet."

Helpless rage thrashes inside me. "Why would he even want to see me, if what you're telling me is true? If I'm only a body attached to the violin that he used? He can't use me anymore."

"Samantha."

"No one was ever going to kidnap me to get back at my dad, were they? That was just something you said to control me." I'm hurting and angry, and Liam is the only person here. My voice comes out as a shriek. "That was a lie."

He sounds calm. "I don't know exactly what your father wants with you. I could ask him, but I wouldn't take the time. If he's six feet away from me, there's already a bullet in his forehead."

A flinch. I don't want to miss a father who never loved me. I don't want to yearn for my guardian, either. It's a terrible thing, to be a girl alone in the world. It makes me want and want and want, until the wanting is so big it swallows me whole.

I turn away from Liam and walk to the window. The glass cools my palms. The weather must have taken a turn. Or maybe it isn't the outside that's cold. Maybe it's the building itself, stirred from a deep slumber, chilled by the shadows in the room.

The warmth behind me can only be Liam's body. The comfort I always needed. Always wanted. Even now, when he's torn into my deepest fears and made them real. "You never used me," I whisper, because no one could mistake the way he turned his life over for me. The only question is why? My own flesh-and-blood father didn't care about me. Why did Liam North?

His hands land on my shoulders. Slowly, slowly, as if I'm made of porcelain, he pulls me back into a hug. Maybe the first one he's ever given me. Maybe the first one he's ever given *anyone*. He doesn't seem to know where to put his hands. Or how to hold his body. He would almost surely feel more comfortable scaling a mountain or fighting a mountain lion.

I took care of you for six years. You never needed anything.

Except a hug!

He's doing it now, but it feels like it's too late. I'm already formed this way, as awkward as him with physical comfort. It makes me want to punish him. I rock my hips back against him, and yes, *yes*, he's hard against my ass. He sucks in a breath. "I did use you," he mutters.

"Use me again."

He holds himself very still. It's a refusal, that stillness. An immovable mountain. Except that when I roll my hips against him, I feel the way he cracks. He feels impossibly hard against the soft flesh of my ass. As if he's made of stone warmed in the desert sun. His erection throbs against me. It's the only sign of weakness.

The only sign of humanity.

I lean my head back until it rests against his chest, tucked into the crook of his neck. He drops his lips to my temple, and I feel his anguish in every breath. His determination to give me pleasure while holding himself in check. "Keep your hands there."

Every muscle in my body clenches tight. He's really going to do it. He's going to touch me. Maybe fuck me. Was he hoping for this when he gave the name Fritz Kreisler at the front desk? Was he thinking about my body? The answer comes in the form of his hands. They aren't gentle. One grasps my breast, the way a starving man would food. He doesn't caress me. He *holds* me. His other hand keeps my hips still. "You like to tease me?" he whispers. "You like rubbing your ass on my cock? Making me insane?"

"Yes," I moan, not caring if he punishes me. Wanting him to.

His lips brush the side of my neck—once, twice. So soft it's almost a breath. He opens his mouth, a kiss in a place so sensitive it makes me shiver. A discordant *squeak* as my hands slide an inch down the glass. "Keep your hands on the window," he says again. "Or I'll stop touching you."

I force myself to focus on the jagged landscape of downtown Tanglewood, overcast clouds bearing down on peaked steel and glass. There's an entire city in front of me, but I can only think about the man behind me. He still grasps me, too rough, artless, as if he's afraid I might escape from these self-imposed restraints. His lips nibble my earlobe, and sensation pools between my legs. How is it possible? He traces his tongue along the shell of my ear. It feels more intimate than sex.

By slow degrees he makes himself loosen his hold on my breast. One hand slides under my shirt. He groans when he finds no bra to block his way. His palm covers my nipple, rubbing in large circles, surprisingly gentle. My nipples tighten into aching points. Pain gathers between my legs, a mixture of frustration and want. My hands curl into fists against the glass. He stops immediately. His hands don't move. They're held against me in silent reprimand, waiting for me to flatten my palms again. Once I do, he rewards me with a nip to my shoulder. I jump, rocking back against his cock.

"Please," I whisper. "Please, please, please."

He slips his other hand beneath my skirt and under my panties, finding the slick folds. "Such a sweet little cunt. I can't stop thinking about it. When I should be working, I'm thinking about how warm you are, how wet. How pinching your little clit makes you moan."

I'm mindless with desire, my eyelids at half-mast, my hips moving in restless supplication. He plays with me as if plucking the strings of a violin, each one a small surprise, the tempo too slow for me to come. "Have sex with me," I whisper.

"No, no. You have to say the words, *Please fuck me, Liam.*"

My lips tremble. Tears stream down my face. They aren't about sadness. He's stretched my body to what it can bear. "Please... please fuck me, Liam."

Two fingers slip inside me, and I gasp. "Is this what you meant?"

"N-no."

"You should be more specific, sweetheart. Now you're going to have to get yourself off like this, pressing your clit against my hand until you come. I want you to squeeze my fingers tight enough to break them. I want to feel you dripping down your leg."

A meaningless sound escapes me, one of hunger. I want his cock inside me, but I'm too far gone to say the words. He strums me faster and faster, until I'm vibrating with pleasure.

I'm almost too far gone to understand the words he murmurs against my skin, but they filter into my consciousness almost by osmosis, as if we're melding into one. "Love this sweet little body, love the way you need me. Love you. Fuck, I love you."

That's how I come, with his lips pressed

against my neck, his hand grasping my breast, his fingers deep in my sex, pumping with impossible friction, hurtling me over the edge.

When I first held a violin, when I touched a bow to the strings, it felt like speaking for the first time. Like I'd lived in silence and finally found words. I'm a grown woman now, on the cusp of a global musical tour. I have money and independence and even a curious sort of power in the world—but I still feel voiceless without the four hundred grams of wood in my arms. Liam North is the exception. When he touches me, I feel my whole body sing. The notes fill the air even if he steals my breath. A violin is not a thing—not to someone who plays like me. It's moody and emotional and mysterious. That's what Liam is to me. He makes me feel strong. A flush darkens his cheeks. His eyelids droop low. Rough breath widens his nostrils. He's a wild animal, completely untamable—and he's at my fingertips. "On the bed," I say, the command coming out soft.

He doesn't move. "You want more?"

Of his hands on me. His mouth on me. He can make me feel absolute bliss, while trying to keep himself apart. I'm the musician. It's my job to make him sing. "I want you to get on the bed."

This isn't our relationship. I'm not the one

who gives the orders. In the house back in Kingston, he's the commander of our little battalion. Of me—and also Josh and Elijah and everyone who works for North Security.

In this hotel room, in this moment, I'm turning the tables.

LIAM

SHE'S IMPOSSIBLY SMALL and delicate. I want to wrap her in gauze.

Even the air is too rough for her peach-pink skin. My calloused hands probably left bruises on her soft little clit. There is no way she can move me. Slender arms and wide Bambi eyes. There's no way she can physically get me on that bed, but she asked me…and I will deny her nothing. Not even my obedience.

When she takes a step toward me, I take a step back.

Another. Another, until the backs of my legs bump the frame.

She touches her forefinger to the center of my chest. The weight of a butterfly wing. An earthquake in my ribs. I let myself fall back onto the bed, sweat-damp clothes against crisp white sheets. She tugs at the hem of my shirt, and I have to bite back a groan. Her gaze burns a path across my abs. I yank the T-shirt over my head and toss it across the room. That makes her frown. "The bed. Hold on to the bed."

I glance behind me. Scrollwork on brass. She wants me to keep my hands there? My instincts scream to fight. Maintain control. I'm never going back down to the fucking well, never going to be scrabbling against the wet, crumbling stone. It takes more trust than I'm really ready for to breathe in deep and grasp the cool metal. My lips pull back into a snarl. I know my eyes challenge her. Threaten her? She doesn't look cowed.

A small smile curves her lips as she traces a finger over my wrists. "Like tying down a wolf with a string of daisy stems. It should be impossible."

Is that how she sees me? As a wild animal? "Why would you want a wolf?"

"Not just any wolf." She climbs my body, making me grunt in acute arousal. My erection throbs against my workout shorts. "You."

Yes, I picked the name Kreisler hoping that Samantha would find me. Never in my wildest dreams did I imagine I'd be spread out on the bed underneath her, while she straddles me, her slender legs on either side of my hips, her warm sex against my cock. She leans forward, resting her palms on my chest. I suck in a breath. "God, sweetheart. Let me touch you."

She shakes her head, not breaking eye contact. "We're going to play a different game."

I might not survive this. "Tell me what you need."

Lashes brush her cheeks. She keeps her gaze down as she settles more firmly against my cock, her body curving over me like goddamn heaven. "The truth."

A shudder runs through me. "What are you talking about?"

"I'm talking about how you knew my father. How you *really* knew him. Because I know you weren't friends or even colleagues. I know you're keeping secrets."

I reach for her—though what I'd do, I don't know. Push her away? Pull her closer? It doesn't matter because she gives me a stern look. "Don't let go."

The imaginary daisy stems pull taut, and I grasp the bedframe again. "I would never do anything to hurt you. There are things I haven't told you… things I can't tell you."

She rocks her hips over my cock, the warmth of her sex a painful slide on my arousal. I swear in colorful abandon, and she does it again. "Why can't you tell me? Oh, let me guess. Because I'd be in danger. That's always your excuse. Protecting me."

My teeth are gritted against the blinding pleasure of her body. The brass creaks in my fists. It takes every ounce of willpower not to grab her hips and fuck her. "I will never apologize for keeping you safe."

She leans down, letting her hair fall in my face. I breathe in the scent of honey and rosin. "What if you're not keeping me safe, Liam? What if you're putting me in danger by not telling me the whole truth?"

Fuck. A knife in my chest. A warm wash of arousal against my cock. It's too much to hold back. "Let me fuck you," I mutter, tilting my hips to press the head of my cock against her clit. "I'll make you feel so good."

"Not until you tell me the truth. Why did you save me that day?"

"You were a little girl." Which makes what I'm doing wrong—every rub of her cunt on my cock. It doesn't matter that she's all grown up. It's still wrong.

"So what? You were the big bad assassin, weren't you? Why not let me die?"

"I don't kill children."

"So then you saved my life. Why did you come look for me in that orphanage? And don't tell me civic duty. I don't believe you. There was no reason to adopt me."

Pleasure shoots through my brain, and I know I only have a few seconds left to hold on to my sanity. She can't know the truth. It's made of flower stems and knotted petals, like the bonds on my wrists—a fragile latticework that can be blown away. "You don't want to do this."

She rubs against my dick, and her eyes flutter closed in pleasure. "I do."

I'm panting, in pain, my entire body shuddering in the throes of this exquisite torture. "The truth, Samantha? You want me to tell you that I fell in love with you when you stood in that freezing fucking square in Leningrad? Or the first time I heard you play?"

Her eyes widen, and she moves, moves, moves on my cock. "*Liam.*"

My control snaps in half, leaving only the animal side of me. I flip her onto her back and tear the seam of her panties. Then my cock is inside her, and I'm rutting like a goddamn animal. I want her smeared in mud while the sky thunders above us. I want mating cries in the treetops at night. "Are you happy now?" I growl against her throat. "Knowing I broke every rule for you. Knowing I'd do it again. I love you, Samantha, and I hate you for it."

She gasps and claws at me, her nails sharp on my shoulders. I don't know whether she's more shocked at my words or at my blunt cock in her tight cunt.

"That's why I got you out of that orphanage. Because I'm fucked up beyond reason. Beyond fixing. Forgive me. God. Samantha, I'm so sorry." And then I'm coming, thrusting into her, blind and battered, my shame exposed, my deepest guilt laid bare to the woman who cries out and clenches and climaxes underneath me.

CHAPTER TWELVE

The pianist Schumann ruined his performing career by using a homemade finger-stretching device while practicing.

LIAM

SUNLIGHT LEAKS THROUGH the heavy brocade curtains. Her eyelids flutter. She stretches against me, which is exquisite agony. I haven't been able to sleep, not when she's back in my arms. Those innocent brown eyes open. They're enough to strip me bare. Every defense I might have. Every hope. When you've lived in that well long enough, it starts to feel like home. That's why I can't let myself keep her—I would only drag her down with me.

I trace her eyebrow and the curve of her cheek. Touching her is like touching sunshine. It shouldn't be possible for someone like me. She shifts, and I glance down at her breasts—so small and perfect, those breasts. One delicate hand reaches for the sheet to cover herself.

"Don't," I say, my voice gravelly.

I may not be able to keep her, but she's here in bed with me. In this moment, she's mine. Her nipples pebble in the cool morning air. A sliver of sunlight leans across her stomach. I lean down and press an open-mouthed kiss, tasting the beam on her skin. She laughs, ticklish, the sound more beautiful than any music a violin could make.

Something heavy shifts in my chest. What the fuck am I doing? She should be with someone like that Harry March. She should be with someone young and playful, someone who doesn't dream about drowning in the dark.

I give the gold alarm clock a pointed look. "You should probably get back to your room."

Her eyes widen. "Oh. I thought maybe we could…spend the day together?"

If there was blood sprayed across the white sheets it would make sense to me. That's how it feels, as if I've been sliced open. She can't know how vulnerable she makes me. She can't know how dangerous that is. "You've probably had enough orgasms for now."

That's me, the responsible guardian, always watching out for her best interests. She should always have the right amount of electrolytes and vitamins and orgasms. The silence shimmers with her hurt. It would be so easy to kiss her. To fuck her. To lose myself in her body until I forgot all about deep, dark wells. That would be the worst thing for her. More cruel than staying silent as she stands and gets dressed in last night's clothes.

The walk of shame. She's going to do the walk of shame back to her hotel suite. That's what I've done to her. All I can think about is fucking her again.

She pauses at the door. "What are you going to do?"

I'm going to jack off imagining her pouty lips and velvet nipples. I'm going to ache every goddamn second that she's away from me. "About what?"

"About the note."

Yes, the fucking note. The idea of her father getting that close to her makes my whole body seize up. Where is he hiding? He's somewhere in Tanglewood. Damon Scott came through with solid information, but by the time I got to the motel he'd been using, he was already gone. "I'm going to find out how he got close to you. And then I'm going to finish the job I started years ago."

Her nod is solemn. There won't be any reason for me to chase after her once she's safe. No reason for me to follow her tour around the world. I'm not sure how I'll survive it; I only know that she deserves to be free of the past. I'm part of her past.

I open the door for her, unsurprised to find Josh waiting outside.

He raises his eyebrows. "You kids have fun?"

Samantha's cheeks turn pink. "Could you maybe pretend you didn't see this?"

"Not a chance."

I touch two fingers to Samantha's arm. "Wait at the end of the hall, sweetheart. I need to talk to this asshole about your security." Only when she's gone do I turn to my brother. "He got to her."

"What do you mean?"

"I mean her father left a fucking note in her violin case at the theater."

He curses. "How?"

"That's what I want to know?"

Dark eyebrows rise. "You making an accusation, big brother?"

"I'm saying you let him get way too fucking close."

He's quiet a moment. His eyes are a darker green than mine, almost eerie. "Maybe he's not the only one getting too close to her."

"Aren't you the one who said I should fuck her?"

"Fuck her. Not fall for her."

His words stay with me the rest of the day. I'm so distracted by the memory of her pussy, by my addiction to it, that I almost miss the flicker in his eyes. *You making an accusation, big brother?* I meant that he needed to guard her better, but someone got past our defenses. The security systems and the protection. Someone probably had help. *The human element.* We talked once about the human element when it came to Samantha.

Every single person was a weak link. Even my own brother.

You making an accusation, big brother?

If someone had betrayed me, I had to consider that it had come from my family. I had to consider it could be Josh.

CHAPTER THIRTEEN

By the Pope's order, Miserere mei was only played in the Sistine Chapel during certain ceremonies. A fourteen-year-old Mozart listened to it twice and wrote it down by memory—the first time it had ever left the church.

JOSH

HAUNTING VIOLIN MUSIC beats against my back as I leave the stage. Five silver strings and a few strands of catgut makes a sound loud enough to fill every inch of this theater. That's one upside to guarding a classical violinist—I can hear her even on my rounds.

Tweedledee and Tweedledum have disappeared for the day. That's what I call the reps from the recording label. Apparently Harry fucking March started a brawl in a club last night, so they're over there with their black-suit legal guys, probably writing a big check. That means Samantha is on her own to practice onstage.

Christ. This tour. I'll be happy when it's over.

It's not that I don't appreciate her talent. It's

world class. But you won't ever find me with tickets to the symphony. That's my brother. Liam lives like a monk—no fucking, no drinking, no red meat. He probably gets off on watching the angle of his little girl's arm as she draws a long note. Me? I enjoy steaks and whiskey.

And I really enjoy women.

There are men stationed outside the Grand. I'll get a text if anyone on the pre-approved list comes inside. A phone call and a chance to vet them myself if it's someone new. That doesn't mean I ease up on my rounds. Every hour I take a tour through the warren of hallways and rooms backstage. Which is how I end up outside the dance room.

A low, rhythmic, almost tribal bass emanates from the recessed speakers. Bethany wears a black leotard and pale pink ballet shoes. Her partner is nowhere in sight. She moves with an athletic grace through a series of bends and turns on the parquet floor. It's too primal to be called a dance. Too beautiful not to be. She vaults herself into a perfect pirouette before settling lightly on her feet. It doesn't mistake my notice that Samantha plays a song that isn't from the show, something far deeper and more haunting than anything they make her play. Bethany's dance isn't part of the show, either. I don't think the label reps have any idea the scope of the talent they're dealing with.

I choose that moment to step into the room. Mirrors on every wall make it look like there are twenty of me. Bethany lets out a little shriek and whirls to face me. "What are you doing here?"

Her voice sounds like poetry, the lilt at the ends of her words, the accent on her vowels. I recognized it immediately, though it's clear she's tried to erase it. "You're from Louisiana, aren't you? Were you there for Hurricane Katrina? You must have been a little girl."

Pretty brown eyes narrow. "God, you're an asshole."

The sooner she really understands that, the less surprised she'll be. "Did they carry you through the water? Or did you have to swim?"

"I should tell the label that you're saying this shit. They'd kick you out."

"And lose their Alice in Wonderland in the process? Not likely."

She makes a face. "The only reason I haven't said anything to Samantha is because she'd be upset. I know she thinks of you like family. For what reasons, I have no idea."

We're not family. My brothers are my family. I would kill for them. Though the killing's easy.

Dying would be harder. I'd do that, too. Samantha? I'll protect her, but only for my brother's sake. I care about the violin prodigy, but to me she'll always be the twelve-year-old girl with wide, lost eyes. She'll always be a sign of my brother's weakness.

Nothing like the woman standing in front of me.

I take a step forward and circle her, admiring the curve of her ass and the glisten of sweat on her skin. She pushes herself so hard. It doesn't matter what the label reps throw at her. *Harder. Faster. Do it again.* They make her work for hours, and she does it without pause.

Of course it makes my dick hard. I like to work a woman over in bed. I like to hit it hard. A compliant little doll with the body of an athlete? She's basically my dream woman.

"Speaking of family," I say, leaning close to breathe in her salt and sweetness. "How does yours feel about you following in their footsteps?"

She stiffens. "I'm not a stripper. And what the hell are you doing looking into me?"

"I have dossiers on all the tour members, which means I know so many dirty little secrets. For example, your dance partner. There was that small incident in Colombia."

Her eyes flash as she faces me, highlighting the emerald flecks in her pupils. "Leave him alone."

"Don't tell me you have a crush on Romeo. Such a waste, considering he wouldn't return it."

"He's a good person, and he doesn't deserve you talking shit about him."

"What about you? Are you a good person?" My voice mocks her, because of course she is. She tries so hard to be good, which should be a turn-off. Instead it makes me want to teach her how to be bad.

Her chin lifts. "This is a private rehearsal. You need to leave. And besides, you aren't here to guard me. You're here for Samantha."

Yes, I'm here for Samantha Brooks. Violin prodigy. World-class musician. I'll keep her alive because Liam wants that. The second she's safe, I'm coming for my pretty little dancer. She'll stand in the music box I make for her, spinning and spinning, her posture perfect, arms poised above her head so I can touch her everywhere.

CHAPTER FOURTEEN

The composer Wagner had a huge influence over Hitler, who loved Wagner's music, and then became enthralled with his anti-Semitic writings.

SAMANTHA

A CART COVERED in a white tablecloth and silver domes waits in the corner. The idea of vegetable tartine and pomme frites turns my stomach. I should definitely eat, but every muscle clenches tight. I'm not sure I could force a bite past the knot in my throat.

Two months of practice have led to this moment—the night before the premiere. My stomach turns, and I think I'd throw up if I'd managed to eat anything today. This is what being grown up feels like. This is what independence looks like. Doesn't it?

In some ways my carefully defined box has moved from Liam's house to the constraints of the tour. Am I still a ward, the record label my new guardians? This is what I was working toward, but now that it's in my reach, I don't know if there's any freedom in it.

There's a soft knock at the door.

I open it expecting to see Josh or maybe Beatrix coming down to visit. Instead it's Laney from back home. I can't help the laugh of surprise that escapes me. I throw my arms around her and squeeze, breathing in the familiar warmth. "What are you doing here?"

Only vaguely do I see Liam watching us with that usual aloofness, his expression set in grim lines, only the faintest flicker of affection turning his lips. "She has front-row tickets tomorrow."

I give her an accusing look, making my voice sound like hers. "Oh no, I couldn't possibly travel right now. There's study groups and football games and fun college things to do."

She grins at me, unrepentant. "There's so many fun college things to do, but none of them even come close to watching you become a superstar."

"Ha! I'm going to fall on my face, and you're going to watch it live."

Pain lances my side as she pinches me in retribution. "Hey, I'm not going to let you talk about my friend like that. She's the *star* of this Alice in Wonderland-themed show."

Liam clears his throat. "I'll wait outside."

I give him a curious look. "Where's Josh? He never came back."

"He's gone."

"What do you mean, gone?"

Hard as a diamond. His expression reveals nothing but angles and depth. "I'm going to head up your security detail from now on."

Holy shit. He wouldn't do that to Josh. It's a clear sign that he doesn't trust him... except looking at Liam's deep-green eyes, that's exactly how it looks. There's a bleakness lurking at the back of his gaze. "Don't I get a say in this? It's my security."

I don't really expect him to consult with me. There's respecting me as a woman. And then there's keeping me safe. He'll chain himself to the bed if I ask it, but he won't hesitate to throw himself in front of me if there's a bullet heading my way. That's not something I can change in him any more than I can change his DNA.

Mostly I say it so he'll tell me what's going on. Where *is* Josh?

"No," Liam says simply, and then calmly, almost gently, closes the door in my face.

"Oh my God," I tell the wood paneling.

Sometimes my love for Liam North is the

hardest thing. The worst thing. Isn't love supposed to be a blessing? Not when you love a controlling, stubborn, emotionally closed man. Even when I try to stand up to him, it doesn't work out the way I planned.

Only during sex does he seem to open up to me at all.

"What the *hell* has been going on in Tanglewood?" Laney says, munching on a French fry from the room service cart. "I feel like I've missed all the fun."

"Did your mom tell you anything?"

Laney takes a bite of the tartine and then makes a face. "Whoever first decided to get cheese from a goat should be shot. Also, yes. She told me that Josh's clearance got pulled."

My mouth drops open. "In North Security? He's one of the owners!"

She slides onto the couch and covers her eyes. "There's a mole."

"No way." I sit down next to her and grasp her hands, forcing her to look at me. "There's no freaking way that Josh would do anything like that."

A doubtful look. "He's kind of an asshole."

"Of course he's an asshole. That doesn't mean he would do anything to hurt Liam."

She's quiet a moment. "Are you really the star of the show?"

"No. I mean, maybe. Harry March is the headliner. That is never going to change, but my part is a lot more than I thought it would be. I figured I'd play a song or two. Not have this acting thing throughout the whole show. It's honestly… terrifying."

Blue eyes meet mine. "Josh wouldn't do anything to hurt his brothers, that's true. He loves them. What if he thought you were the one hurting them?"

My loyalty is to my brother. Not you. "He knows I love Liam."

"What if you didn't mean to? What if your very existence threatens Liam?"

My stomach churns. "This night was a lot easier when I was only worried about falling on my face tomorrow. Josh is like family to me. If I can't trust him, who can I trust?"

"He probably doesn't want you to die."

"Surprisingly, this isn't helping."

"I'm just saying, let Liam take care of you."

That makes me sigh. "Liam has never had a problem taking care of me. Protecting me, feeding me. Ordering me around. It's the other stuff that makes him a little crazy."

Her eyes light up. "So you *have* been doing other stuff?"

My cheeks heat. "No."

"Liar liar liar. Tell me all about it."

"There may have been a night in his hotel room." A night where he made me come and held me down. Where he confessed that I almost died at age twelve because of poison he planted.

"What about Harry March?" she asks with a sly smile.

I make a face. "What about him?"

"Is he as wild as everyone says?"

That makes me pause. There's more than wildness in him. Something deeper than a playboy. A chasm at the very core. "He's worse." I remember the look in his eyes as he pressed his foot on the gas. It was like he had a death wish. "I honestly don't know how this tour is going to go, Laney. Sometimes it feels a little bit doomed."

CHAPTER FIFTEEN

Mozart finished writing the overture to Don Giovanni the morning the show opened. It took hours for the copyists to write out the score. The orchestra had no time to rehearse. They had to sight-read the music.

SAMANTHA

SET DESIGNERS HAVE been working for weeks, but it always looked like a stage. Tonight the Grand is a forest. Deep shadows surround bursts of spotlighted foliage. Blinking eyes made from discreet temporary lights peek from beneath heavy green leaves.

I suppose I'm one pair of blinking eyes, from my hiding place behind the curtain. Couples enter from the back, glittering in evening gowns and tuxes. The theater is darker than it normally would be before a show. It's a concession to the theme—one of many. It makes even the guests look like part of the glittering, dramatic backdrop.

It's hard to believe this many people will soon see me play.

They don't know who I am. It's one thing for a conductor to follow the career of a child prodigy. For the ordinary patron, even one who loves music, I'm just a name in their glossy Playbill. Somehow I'm also the one who's onstage the most. Weird. And terrifying.

Chills race over my skin. Followed by a wash of nervous heat.

My body doesn't know how to regulate its temperature right now.

"It looks amazing," says a voice from behind me, and I whirl to see Candy standing there, wearing a couture gown that probably costs more than a car, looking like she stepped off the red carpet at some Hollywood gala.

I nod my agreement, mostly because my throat is too dry to speak.

"They said it was your idea, the theme."

"Oh no," I manage to croak. The costume that had once felt so foreign now fits me like a second skin. Hours of rehearsals, and I'm more comfortable in blue silk and white lace than jeans and a T-shirt. "I mean, yes, but the idea came from the building. And from the painting by Harper St. Claire at the entrance. That was the inspiration."

Candy smiles. "I'll have to tell her that. She's

in the audience."

My stomach turns over. The famous artist? The one with a billion Instagram followers? Her doodles on cocktail napkins are basically instant masterpieces, and she's going to watch me for the first time onstage. I'm going to fall flat on my face. "Oh God."

"Don't worry, honey. Everyone's rooting for you."

A moan escapes me. "You won't be saying that if I throw up onstage."

Candy peeks past the velvet curtain, her cool blue eyes assessing the crowd. She doesn't have to go onstage, but I have the sense that if she did, she wouldn't be fazed. "Can I give you some advice?"

"Does it involve you playing Alice instead of me?" I ask hopefully. "You have the blonde hair and the blue eyes and you almost definitely won't pass out."

That earns me a small smile. "I'm afraid I'd already seen too much before I ever entered this particular forest." She tugs gently on a curled lock of my hair. "You might have beautiful black hair and tanned skin, but you're far more of an authentic Alice."

I make a face. "Does that mean I'm naïve?"

"It means you're properly wary of the dangers

of the world, but still curious enough to go wandering. Don't let anyone tell you different—Alice didn't stumble onto magic. She created it."

"I always thought she had more power than people gave her credit for."

A knowing look. "Every woman does."

A thousand butterflies still swarm my stomach, but I have a sense that I'm meant to do this. That it's worth the terror. "Thank you for the pep talk."

She gives a delicate cough. "Yes, well, that wasn't my real advice. My real advice comes from the days when I stood on this stage and took off my clothes."

My mouth forms a delicate O. "Is it to imagine the audience naked?"

"Absolutely not. Whatever you do, don't do that."

That makes me giggle, which shouldn't have been possible at a moment like this. The lights dim and brighten, dim and brighten, dim and brighten, telling the audience to find their seats. The show is about to begin. "What's your real advice?"

"The men in that audience, they don't want your nakedness. That's available for far less money in an alleyway not far from here. They want what you're hiding, which means you have to keep something hidden. They want the secrets. They want the mystery."

There's a pang in my heart, because Candy sounds so wise, but she can't be that much older than me. It hurts to think of her learning these lessons that young. Did she have a choice when she started stripping? There are depths in her blue eyes that answer the question. *No.* "What was your secret?"

There's no mistaking the Mona Lisa smile she gives me. She may not tell me her secrets, but she's showing them to me. This is what it feels like to watch her hide something, to want it for yourself, to be spellbound. I don't think I have that kind of mastery, whether my clothes are off or on.

She leans close enough that I have the faint scent of cherry blossom on my tongue. "My secret was that I danced for only one man. We aren't so different, you and I. You play for only one man."

The sound of a single violin comes from the orchestra pit. A signal that the show has begun. The entire stage turns dark. I know from memory that the spotlight will appear on me when I step onto the stage. Candy gives my hand a silent squeeze before slipping away.

It feels like everyone in the theater is holding their breaths. Maybe even the building itself. Waiting, waiting. I've missed my cue. They can't begin without me. I close my eyes. *You play for only one man.* Is that true? In the literal sense it was true when I practiced for hours every day in the music room adjacent to his office.

And in the figurative sense…

I could make a fool of myself in front of thousands of people tonight. Reporters from national newspapers sit in the press box, ready to shout my disasters from the rooftops. If I fall on my face, I'll probably be a social media spectacle by lunchtime tomorrow.

There's only one man whose opinion really matters. He's watching me from his position backstage. There are men and women from North Security stationed around the entire building, forming a net of protection. A thousand things could go wrong tonight, but only one man has the power to make things right. From the corner of my eyes I can see the label reps waving me onto the stage. Liam looks like he could wait all night, with complete patience and utter calm.

The corner of my lips turns up in a smile. This is what Candy meant. Making them wait. Making them wonder. What kept her so long?

With that thought fresh in my mind, I take a step onto the stage. White light blinds me. I can't see anyone in the audience. It doesn't matter. The seats could be empty. I give the performance of my life, wandering into the forest, finding mysterious creatures, changing in ways I couldn't have imagined.

A wild thing happens. The audience laughs when they're supposed to laugh. They clap when they're supposed to clap. They gasp when Harry March makes his appearance twenty feet above the stage, his purple suit and taunting grin a delightful surprise.

I suppose it should be obvious that if we re-hearse enough times we'd be able to do the show, but it still feels shocking to me. Shocking enough that when I stumble into a garden of talking flowers and pick up my violin and bow, the music comes out like a breath I've been holding—long and glad.

The Mendelssohn Concerto is possibly the greatest concerto ever written. It was one of the first to allow the soloist to begin, in an agile and lyrical tune. The orchestra joins the conversation next, led by Mr. Ocha in flawless execution. It's a bastardized version we're playing. The label reps didn't want to spend thirty minutes, regardless of its brilliance. But, as I lean into the slow tempo of the second act, I know this was the right piece to play. Fast and slow. Fast and slow. It has the audience spellbound as much as it does me. *This* is what it means to perform. Not only to play a song, but to invite the audience inside.

I lift my gaze on the final note, imagining that I can see Liam behind me. God knows I can feel him. It awakens parts of my body. My nipples against the lace. The place between my legs, warm and secret. How is it possible to stand in front of a thousand people but feel something private? Is this the mystery Candy was talking about?

During the second act Bethany and Romeo somersault their way onto the stage. They represent Alice's irreverent curiosity—to drink what says, *drink me.* To eat what says, *eat me.* To grow large and small and then large again. They are both strong and helpless to the human urges, a perfect counterpoint of cause and effect.

Harry strolls across the stage, singing an up-beat song from his latest album about disappearing and then reappearing, that megawatt grin blinding, his long-limbed grace more sensual as the crowd claps. Then it's Bea's turn to play the beautiful baby grand onstage, her own arrange-ment of a song from Stevie Nicks's album The

Other Side of the Mirror, about dreams and magic and heartbreak.

For a few minutes it seems like we'll actually pull it off. It feels like I've actually created this magic, somehow, through wonder and wandering, following a white rabbit down the hole.

The stagehands hook the invisible silver strings to the harness hidden in the ruffles. When I take the next step onto the stage, I'm pulled high off the ground. The audience gasps as I soar above them. My own breath catches. We've practiced this, but it's different to do it with people below me instead of empty seats. Hopefully they're not seeing anything more than white ruffled petticoats if they look up. The label reps wanted me to play the violin as I soared through the air, but I convinced them that would be a bad idea—mostly because the hefty insurance premium for the Stradivarius doesn't include playing while flying.

Instead I'm to soar in a wide arc over the audience, dazzling them with my pretend-ballet moves. Harry as the Cheshire Cat will capture me, bringing me back down to earth. I take my tour across the stage, feeling the strings strain at the weight and centrifugal force. Then I'm swooping back toward the stage, my arms outstretched.

That's when I realize something is wrong.

I'm about five feet away from Harry when I see that he's sweating. His eyes are glassy. Is he sick? Realization sinks in my stomach. He's not sick. He's high on something. Weed? Cocaine? I have no freaking clue, but this is a really bad time.

He reaches out to catch me—too late.

Wind rushes across my face. I'm passing only centimeters away from him, everything about this is wrong, wrong, wrong. This close I can hear him curse under his breath. And then the orbit yanks me away from him again, sending me out into an unplanned spin over the audience. Everyone who's worked on the show knows this is wrong. The audience doesn't know. They give a satisfying gasp as I swing over them a second time.

Harry lunges for me this time, but our timing is way off. So is his depth perception. He grabs the ruffles of my skirt and pulls. A tearing sound makes me squeak. Oh God. How am I supposed to fix this? This wasn't something we rehearsed. Harry was supposed to catch me. Harry was to not be high.

On the fourth circuit, the audience starts to worry. I can hear their murmurs, feel their stares. This is the dark side of mystery, when there's truly something kept secret.

As I curve back toward the stage, I angle my

legs to change the course of my approach. Instead of reaching toward Harry, I turn toward the baby grand piano. *I'm going to crash directly into it.* All this time I was worried about tripping on my face or throwing up. Turns out the biggest worry is running into a piano while going so fast I hear the whistle of wind behind me. My knee knocks against the lip of the keys. I wince against the pain as my body cants forward. My feet land in unceremonious bunches of piano keys. *Bam. Bam. Bam.* Before I land on the keys with my ass. A very loud sound. Without pause I whip myself around and play a handful of conclusive notes from the Mendelssohn Concerto, harkening back to it, making it seem as if I'd planned to play those notes all along.

Then I stand and take a small bow. The crowd erupts into wild applause. They're standing, even though the show isn't over. It looked like something I did on purpose. As if I kept myself from Harry March, choosing to bring myself down to earth.

Philip Glass's Violin Concerto 1 is a controversial piece. I'm sure that's why the record picked it for the tour. Is it hypnotic? Or grating? You can find music experts who will argue either side. It's the classical world equivalent of Madonna kissing

Britney. Designed to get people talking.

Here in this moment it feels right, as if Glass wrote it just for me to play on this stage of death-defying feats and wild color. There's no denying the energy in the piece. The exultation. It comes through every stroke of the violin, more real than it did during rehearsal, with such fervor that I feel like I'm part of the stage, the audience—that I'm sending every vibration through the building itself. It feels like the Grand is dancing.

SAMANTHA

THE REST OF the show tumbles along with the same exuberance.

Dierdre sings a solo piece wearing a gorgeous red gown, the Queen of Hearts passing her judgment on me as I play a counterpoint along with the orchestra. I'm riding a high I didn't even know existed. There is something more than playing the violin, and I've found it tonight. When the curtains rise for the final bow, the applause shakes the stage.

It's only when I skip offstage and see the faces of the label reps do I realize that something has gone wrong. Staci looks worried. Tracy looks furious. The white-haired man waits with a grim expression. Stagehands dart around handling the final closing of the stage. Through the red curtain I can hear the bustle of the audience leaving. It's only been moments since the magic of that performance, and I'm shivering from the sudden drop.

"Is this your idea of a joke?" the white-haired man asks. I have to force myself to remember his name. He hasn't even been to rehearsals since the first night.

"Mr. Pomphrey," I squeeze out. "I'm sorry."

"Don't fucking apologize," Harry says, his voice probably loud enough to be heard through the red curtain. "I'm the one who couldn't catch you to save my life. Or yours, apparently. Lucky for all of us you knew how to improvise."

Somehow, Mr. Pomphrey grows even more severe. "Do you think it's a good idea to cover for her, Mr. March? Your position is not guaranteed either."

My mouth drops open. Harry just admitted he was the one at fault, but they don't believe him. Now they're threatening both of us. Is there some kind of instant replay? They must know it was Harry who missed the cue. Except it feels like I'm making excuses in the face of his blame. "The show went great," I say, my voice small. "No one in the audience knew anything was wrong."

"How would you know, Ms. Brooks? Have you managed hundreds, thousands of shows? No, because you're only a child. Not a very bright one, if you don't know how important it is to follow the performance you've practiced."

Tears prick my eyes. I hate that I might cry in front of him. I could shout my defense—that Harry was too drunk to catch me the way he did in rehearsals—but it doesn't matter. I don't think this man would believe me. Or care. God, let him fire me. That would almost be better than this, this feeling of utter disbelief. That I could go from the highest moment of my professional career to this—being insulted by an asshole in a suit, who as far as I know doesn't even play an instrument.

One of the extras slams into me from the side, muttering a quick apology before running toward the back. It's a madhouse here. Do shows usually explode after the final curtain falls? Maybe they do. Mr. Pomphrey is right that I don't have experience with shows. I need to be alone in my dressing room so I can process this and figure out where to go from here. Where is Liam? He was here during the show. I saw him.

Mr. Pomphrey lectures me, his voice fading to an insistent drone. My chest squeezes. It's too much. The terror when Harry couldn't catch me. The elation when I made it work. The disappointment that it still wasn't enough. I suppose I could have gone *splat* against the back of the Grand, and they still would have complained about me not following the script.

I turn blindly away, but Harry catches my arm. "I'm sorry," he says, his voice low. "I know I fucked up. I'll talk to him, make sure he understands it was my fault."

His breath wafts over me, something almost biscuity and almond. Memories fire up out of nowhere. My father drinking late at night, a bottle of heavy whiskey on his desk. Was he worried about the secrets he kept? Did he feel any guilt for involving me in it with my violin?

My sadness is a thousand years old. Maybe this is what Liam meant when he said I remembered more than I thought. Except I don't want these memories. "I never saw you drink before," I say to Harry. "Not like this."

He gives me a lopsided smile that makes him look young. Almost boyish. "I'm always wasted when I'm onstage. It's a performance anxiety thing."

He's lying. I don't know how I know, but I do. He was so calm and cool and comfortable in the interview. It's not the same thing, but there wasn't even a hint of anxiety lurking in those dark eyes. "But I saw you during rehearsals. You were so comfortable onstage."

"Rehearsals don't count for shit. Which I guess you know, since I caught you every single time during rehearsals. You could have died today."

I want to reassure him that it wasn't that serious, but it was. That trick with the wires could have gone very wrong if I hadn't managed to land on my own. My spin over the audience is nothing close to the fancy acrobatics that Bethany and Romeo do, but it still requires my partner to be on point. If I'd fallen onto the audience or hit the wall going fifteen miles per hour, this night could have ended in the hospital. Or the morgue.

Harry's holding on to my wrist. Too tight. Too hard. I pull away, wincing at the flash of pain as my skin twists. It feels like everything is backward right now. The audience was ecstatic over our performance, but the record label is ready to fire me. Harry March is the headliner, but he can't go onstage without being wasted. There's no other word for what I need: escape. I flee to the safety of my dressing room, fighting the panic in my chest. Someone sits at my vanity, his body overlarge in the metal-wire chair. For a second, I think it's Liam. I expect to see those warm green eyes in the mirror. Instead they're brown—like mine.

The man turns to face me. My father. He's holding a gun.

CHAPTER SIXTEEN

*Haydn's Symphony No. 96 is nicknamed "The Miracle"
because the audience dodged a chandelier that fell from the
ceiling at the premiere.*

SAMANTHA

MY THROAT ACHES. "What are you doing
here?"

It's such an ordinary question for such a not-ordinary moment. Alistair Brooks is supposed to be dead. The twelve-year-old girl shivering in a Russian orphanage, clinging to her violin like a life raft, would have been overjoyed to find her father alive. The grown woman, who knows her father to be a spy, does not feel joy. There's hurt and fear and grief.

Maybe it's because he looks so different from the man I knew. My father wore suits with double-breasted vests and jacquard ascots. He kept his goatee and eyebrows trimmed. Every-thing he wore and was packed in the collection of high-end luggage that followed us around. Even his coffee came in sealed little tins. This man looks faintly wild. I'm not sure I would have recognized him walking down the street. It's the eyes that give him away. Dark and glittering and completely without remorse.

"I'm here to see my daughter on her opening night, as any father would want to do."

"Most fathers didn't have a funeral six years ago. There were senators at the funeral. Ambassadors and government officials. A former Secretary of State came."

A faint smile. "She wanted to make sure I was dead."

"I guess you weren't."

Sadness fills his eyes, though I don't know whether I can believe it. "It must come as a shock, the news that I'm still alive. Perhaps you feel betrayed. That I should have found you sooner."

"And done what? You never cut the crusts off my peanut butter and jelly sandwich. You never braided my hair or took me to the library. That was always an aide."

"I wanted to come to you sooner. At first it was dangerous, you understand. Then Liam North was there, trying to turn you against me. It looks like he succeeded."

It's a direct hit. An emotional bullet that finds

its target in the soft, mushy, little-girl corner of my heart. "Am I supposed to trust you now? You're holding a gun."

"I'm not pointing it at you, *chere*. I'm only holding it to defend myself, in case your guardian angel should find us. I don't think he would be so lenient."

Chere. The word brings back memories. That's what he used to call me. It's been so many years, but I still remember the warm pleasure it gave me. I feel it now. "You managed to get past his security now. So why couldn't you contact me years ago?"

"Not his security. His brother's. And I had assistance."

My blood runs cold. "Josh would never do that."

"I don't believe you understand what the North brothers are capable of, but then that's to be expected. They raised you, and so you wish to think the best."

Bitterness burns me from the inside. "Yes, kind of like I believed my father cared about me, when actually he just wanted to use my violin as a way to hide information."

He makes a *tsk* sound. "So poisoned against me. My own daughter."

The tears that threatened to fall in front of the label rep spill over. "You were a spy, Daddy. How could you do that? All those things you said about loving your country—"

"They were all true. They were just about a different country than you thought."

"That's a fine distinction to make." Hysteria rises up—the elation of the show, the crash of the label reps. And now this. "So when you said you loved me, you actually loved my violin case. That makes total sense. No one would call you a liar. Oh no, wait. Me. I would."

"I did love you. I do." He sighs, looking deeply upset. His arms spread wide, a comical request for trust when one hand is still holding a gun. Do I think he'll use it on me? I honestly don't know, which is maybe the most messed-up thing someone can think about her own father. "Would it be too much to ask to have a hug?"

"Are you delusional?" I ask, even though I have to lock my knees against the urge to go to him. To curl into his chest and breathe in his sandalwood and clove scent, to let him murmur to me. *Chere, everything will be all right.* Except it won't be all right. The human heart is as much a spy as he was. Not to be trusted. It tells stories I know better than to believe.

"Yes. You're right." He runs a hand over his face, looking more like my old father. Despite his rough-hewn clothes and the wild grooming of his beard. Despite everything, he looks like Daddy. "I understand why you don't trust me, but I need you to listen. You aren't safe. If I could get to you, then someone else could."

"Why would anyone else even want to?" It isn't a question of disbelief. There was the man who tried to run us off the road in Kingston. The man with a silencer on his gun and no labels on his clothes. An assassin. I believe that I'm in danger; I just don't understand why.

"Because of me. Because of what I did. And as much as I've hated Liam North for the part he played, I've been grateful for one thing—that he kept you safe in Texas. Now that you're touring, you're too accessible. There are people who can be bribed."

"What is this, some kind of retribution for what you did?"

"Retribution? No." His smile is thin. "They want information."

"I don't have any information. The only reason I even knew you were a spy is because Liam told me."

"You know more than you think you do."

"God. I'm tired of hearing that. You sound like Liam now, which is way more disturbing than anything you've said before. I remember more than I think. What are you even talking about?"

"It wasn't something we shared widely, your memory. You could play music. That was enough of a marvel for the world. They didn't know that you could also memorize ten sheets of music at a glance."

I stare at him, stubborn and silent. My memory is not something I've ever talked about. Not with my father. Not even with Liam. I knew it was better than average, but I never *wanted* to talk about it.

"You think Liam doesn't know? Of course he does. He probably knew when he was busy spying on us in Leningrad, well before you came into his care."

There's a rustle outside the door, and I tense—if Liam comes in, this is going to erupt in gunfire. I'm not happy with my father, but I'm not sure I can stand by and watch him be killed either. It doesn't matter. A second later the mirror swings open. My father disappears into a tunnel I didn't know existed. A moment later the door to the dressing room flies open. Liam stands there looking furious. This must be how a town felt when the Vikings landed, prepared to conquer. He could slay a thousand men right now, but there aren't any in the room.

LIAM

I DON'T TRUST anyone. Not the label reps. Not the security who work the Grand. Not even the men and women I brought with me from Kingston. It's me and her on the dark highway, heading away from the theater. Away from L'Etoile where our rooms wait.

"You don't really think it could be Josh, do you? He's your brother."

She looks so damn lost sitting there in that white lace and blue satin costume. I want to rip it to shreds like I'm a wild animal. Isn't that the fucking truth? I glare at her, letting her see the threat in my eyes. Fear shouldn't be so satisfying. "We didn't come from a family with apple pie and baseball, in case you haven't figured that out by now."

"But you own North Security together."

That makes me laugh. It's a cold sound. "I started North Security so people could pay me to hurt people. It turns out my brothers are pretty good at the job, too. I suppose that makes sense.

We were taught by the best."

She looks away. "Your father hurt you?"

The streetlights flash across the windshield in rapid succession. I let the silence answer the question. Of course our father hurt us. All fathers hurt their children. Don't they? It's a ridiculous and inescapable logic to a kid with our upbringing.

All I wanted was not to hurt Samantha. That would have been enough for me. At the pearly gates, with blood on my hands, a thousand fucking sins, I wanted that one thing. That Samantha Brooks had lived a full and happy life because of me.

We're almost to the house when I answer. "It doesn't matter."

"It matters to me. Why won't you tell me? Why do I have to share my feelings and my secrets with you, but you won't do the same for me?"

"He knocked me around. Is that what you want to hear?"

Brown eyes turn bright with tears. "Liam."

"When I couldn't get up anymore, he'd get to work on Josh and Elijah. And sometimes? Sometimes I'd still be conscious. Unable to get up. I'd have to listen."

"He was a monster."

We turn onto gravel. No one knows about the house. The infamous Damon Scott came through with this place, at least. It has a white picket fence. A balcony. Flowers that grow up the side. Whatever she wants I'll find for her. It's not even a choice. It's a biological imperative.

Her eyes turn wide. "Where are we?"

"A safe house."

She glances at the house like it might eat her. "Why?"

Why? Because she's in danger. Because it's my fault. It hurts to be near her. The only thing worse is being apart. "I look just like him—my father. When he held me underwater in the bathtub, when he pushed my hands on the burning stove. When he dropped me into the well, it was his own fucking face he was looking at."

"I'm so sorry," she says, her voice breaking.

"You think I want that? Your sympathy? Your pity?" I step out of the car and cross to the other side, opening her door. "That's the shit that's inside my brain. I keep it away from you because I don't want you to know. We'll stay here until we leave the city."

"It's beautiful," she says, sounding cautious. Cautious because I'm acting like a maniac.

Knowing that doesn't help me stop. He had a gun. The thought blinds me with rage and utter terror. He had a gun. I take her hand and lead her inside, too fast. There's a security system, freshly installed. I close us inside. Lock out the world.

There's a grand piano in the foyer. That was a nice touch.

I back her up against the instrument. It catches her at the hips, and she has to lean back on it, playing a rush of discordant notes. This isn't the pretty music she's used to. "I got big enough to fight back. That should have been the end. I should have pushed him into the well and made sure he never got back out. Instead I kept my head down until I could enlist. I left my brothers to defend themselves."

"Josh loves you." A single tear runs down her cheek. I lean down and kiss the salt-drop into my mouth. I drink down her sorrow the same way I want to eat her pretty little cunt. Her breath blows jagged against my temple. She's afraid of me. *Afraid.*

"Maybe he does love me. Maybe he hates me. Maybe we didn't learn the fucking difference. All we know is how to survive, Samantha. And we will kill anything that threatens that."

Her eyes widen, because she understands the

warning. She's a threat to me. That should be enough to make her run screaming into the woods. God, I'm looming over her like an asshole. I'm caging her in. She should fight me. Instead she reaches for the white-lace straps on her shoulders and pulls them down. I'm mesmerized as her plump breasts appear above the lace. Her nipples look impossibly dark framed like that. "What are you doing?" I ask, my voice hard.

"I don't know," she whispers. "Sympathy? Pity? All the things you claim not to want. Love? I'm loving you."

I lean down and suck her nipple into my mouth, flicking the firm tip again and again, biting it gently between my teeth. "This isn't love. This is fucking. You don't know the difference. You're confused."

She turns over and flips up the blue satin skirts, revealing her white stockings and ruffled panties. Her dark gaze over her shoulder is pure sin. It's Eve taking a bite of the apple. "Then show me the difference." Challenge gives her voice a dark note. "If you're so sure I'm confused, give me a good fuck without loving me."

I'd have to hurt her to prove that.

Have to fuck her cunt hard and fast, before she's ready for me. Fuck her so long she'd be raw and aching. There's nothing on this earth that could compel me to do that. And so I do the only thing left. I kiss the back of her neck. For this moment, I'm hers. The man who loves her— broken and wrong. I taste her skin, this Alice in a costume, this child prodigy who grew up into my worst nightmare. Someone who could make me feel again.

Maybe I'm the one who doesn't know the difference between love and fucking. Maybe I'm the one who's so goddamn confused I can't see straight.

I lead her upstairs and undress her with quiet concentration. She lets me move her this way and that, like she's an acquiescent doll. I let her play the part, but we both know that she's the initiator. She's the one in control. "They say that Alice represents passivity," she murmurs, sounding thoughtful. "That she was Lewis Carroll's representation of a good, timid female."

That gives me pause, despite the riot in my blood. "Is that what you think?"

She sighs, sounding more lost than when she plays the part onstage. "I don't know if that's what he wanted, but it's what I want. Does that make it wrong?"

My cock surges, wanting to prove to her how

very not-wrong it would be to let me lead her. There are sixty bricks that circle the well. There are two hundred that stack, bottom to top. Simple facts that make my blood run cold. That calms my dick for long enough to speak like a human instead of growl at her like an animal. "I want to make you feel good, whether you're sitting on my face and I'm licking your pretty cunt or I'm riding you from behind, covering your mouth with my hand. Anything that will make you come, everything that will make you come."

Her eyes have gone wide, and I think maybe I've fucked it up. Maybe we should go back to arguing about love and sex, except that's even more dangerous ground. It's quicksand. One foot in, and I'm sinking. "I want that," she says, her voice hoarse.

Blood pounds in my temples. "Which one?"

"Both, I think. The first one, too. But mostly… the second one."

Me fucking her from behind, one hand covering her mouth, feeling the vibrations of her moans against my palm. Jesus Christ. I can't hold back anymore. I take her mouth with mine, thrusting my tongue inside, showing her how it will be— crude, that's how it will be. She accepts my roughness with a whimper. *Passivity.* Is this another way that I'm fucked up, wanting her pliant to my invasion? Wanting her to take and take and take?

I'm shaking with the need to slow down, to go gentle. If I were to fuck her like this, it would hurt her. She needs to be wet for this. Swollen and soft. I push my hand between her thighs. Her soft sigh makes me burn. She's wet, but not enough. If I'm going to fuck her from behind, it won't be something I can stop. It won't be something short.

I toss a pillow across the middle of the bed. "Bend over," I tell her, patting the plump cotton. "You're going to need the support by the time I'm done."

There's trust in her eyes. And trepidation. When she doesn't move quickly enough, I bend her over. She looks over her shoulder, and the sight of her in this position makes my cock surge in the cool, conditioned air. I dip two fingers into her warmth. My thumb brushes her clit. She wiggles her ass, already sensitive. I fuck her with my fingers until she clamps down in a soft little climax. Her expression turns drowsy. "Thank you," she murmurs.

"Put your hands on the headboard," I say, waiting until she does. "That was one. You're not nearly ready for me. I'm big, and more important-ly, I'm rough. I'm going to have to fuck you until that pillow is damp underneath. Until your sex is soft enough to let me in."

The clench of her intimate muscles makes me groan. It would feel amazing on my cock, but I can't risk losing control, so I slide two fingers into her cunt and fuck her again to completion. She comes harder this time, clamping down and rocking her hips back to meet me. My cock throbs, wanting inside her heat. "One more time," I mutter. "You can give me that, can't you? You can squeeze my fingers with your pretty pink pussy?"

She moans something unintelligible, tilting her hips to receive me. This woman. I have no fucking defenses against her, and I break my own rules. I notch my cock to her sex and push inside, gasping at the death/pleasure feeling. I slide my hand around to flick her clit and feel her come like a clamp around my dick. I bite down on her shoulder, wanting to punish her for the ache, but it only makes her climax drag on longer.

Only then do I let myself move.

I fuck her with an unbroken rhythm, letting myself experience every inch of friction, every ounce of pleasure. Everything I should have denied myself. She comes with a sudden, shocked cry, but I don't slow down. I ride her through it, and she moans at how sensitive it is. "Again," I mutter, and her body climbs to the peak once again. This time when she comes it's with a keening cry. That's when I cover her mouth with my hand. The muffled sound almost makes me climax, but I force myself to keep going. Sometimes I use physical endurance to punish myself. That's what I'm doing now. It's both a punishment and an endless relief to be fucking this woman, to pump my hips against hers, to feel her ass plush against me. She comes again. This time she collapses onto the bed without holding her position. A kinder man would let her rest. A kinder man wouldn't be fucking her at all. I tilt her hips so I can still access her pussy and keep going. She's sprawled on the bed, her pretty cunt leaving desire damp on my cock. Even exhausted she can't help but respond. Her moans vibrate all the way down to my balls. Minutes pass. Hours. She's everything I ever dreamed of having, everything I've never been allowed to touch. I fuck her until she's collapsed, worn out and sated. Is that the passivity? When she's bent over the bed and fucked out, she can't walk away. Does that mean I want her any way I can get her? There's no denying the obsession I have for Samantha Brooks. No denying the pleasure and the pain that climbs my cock as I pump into her endless, forever. Her mouth is open on the bed, a choked moan moving through the sheets. I press an open-mouthed kiss to her cheek. "I'm going to come," I say, but it's not a command. It's a question.

The gentle squeeze of her secret muscles is the answer, and I spill inside her with a roar that rattles the windows, losing myself to her body, shivering in the aftermath of total surrender.

CHAPTER SEVENTEEN

Opera singer Dame Eva Turner had such a powerful voice that when they recorded her, she had to stand at the back of the orchestra so the instruments could be heard.

SAMANTHA

HARRY MARCH CHARMS AUDIENCE IN WONDERLAND

FALL DOWN THE CLASSICAL MUSIC RABBIT HOLE IN THE HIT NEW SHOW

EAT ME, DRINK ME! CHILD PRODIGY GROWS UP

THE PRESS FOLLOWING opening night is unbelievable—better than any of us expected, more than Harry March got for his past tours. Some combination of the classical music combined with modern pop undertones strikes a chord with the entertainment blogosphere. My photo pops up in surprising numbers, in articles that speculate on my stardom and the rise of the violin in modern culture.

Every single stop on the US tour sells out

within the week.

In the face of such overwhelming success the label reps pretend they planned it that way. Bethany teaches me more moves on the rope line, and I learn to land where I want on the stage by myself—even pulling a few small turns and flourishes while I fly over the audience. This turns out to be an especially good thing, as Harry's drinking increases. His behavior becomes more erratic. At the Seattle show he doesn't arrive until five minutes before the curtain rises. It's hard to leave Beatrix behind, but there's no way she could tour with Madeline—and no way she could leave her behind. We clasp each other in the embellished hallways of L'Etoile while she whispers, "You're the star of this show, Samantha. You deserve to be." I spend the entire ride to the airport in silent tears, trying to reconcile the new life I've fallen into. Because that's how it feels. For all my attempts at independence—it still feels like something that's happening to me.

In the next city we only have the afternoon to practice onstage before the show at seven. It's the tightest rehearsal period yet, and I'm stressed that the rope-line system is different from the ones we've seen before. It's a venue more accustomed to hosting a choir than a concert, so it doesn't have the installations already built. Instead the tour has built something that doesn't look as sturdy as I'd like, not when I'll be relying on it and a partner who shows up three sheets to the wind.

"What is going on with you?" I snap when Harry staggers during part of our back-and-forth dance scene. It's an argument. A fight played out in two-steps and pirouettes. It's the part of the show where Alice demands answers from the Cheshire Cat.

He grins that blinding white smile. "I'm just having a good time. Isn't that what we're here to do? Isn't that why we got into music? Doing what we love. Working the dream."

I make a face at the stench of alcohol he's breathing on me. "You're gross."

"That's what all the girls say," he says solemnly.

"I never see you with any girls, you know that? I thought you're supposed to be a playboy, but all you do is drink alone and then fall asleep somewhere."

"Maybe I'm in love with you."

A shake of my head. I might have believed that at the beginning of the tour—not that he really loved me, but a crush. An infatuation. A simple desire to have sex. At least back then he acted charming to me. He seemed to enjoy my company. The more erratic his behavior, the more withdrawn he's become. We've been in limos and planes together without speaking a word.

"You don't love me. I'm not sure you're sober enough to know who I am."

"I know that I don't want you to die, little violinist."

My pulse spikes. "What the hell does that mean?"

He grabs the rope and steps into the foothold. "It means I have a death wish. Isn't that what you said about me? Life would be so much easier if we could just die."

A kick off the stage, and then he's launched into the air. Turning a wide arc. Flinging out his arms like he's flying. Except he's not hooked into the armhold. He hasn't practiced it like I have. Fear rises in my throat. "Stop that. Get back over here." And then because I can't think of any other way to convince him. "We have to practice."

"I am practicing." He whooshes by me and turns an even larger circle, narrowly missing a beam made of plaster and crown molding. "I'm practicing dying."

Bethany walks onto the stage. "Oh my God.

He's crazy."

"He's not crazy," I say almost absently. I don't know how I know that. He certainly acts crazy, but it feels like something else. "He's hurting."

I spent so many years with Liam North and his band of mercenaries. All of them so desperate to fight, because it seems like the only way they can live.

As if I conjured him with my thoughts, Liam appears. His expression is grim. He takes in the situation in a single glance. Harry watches him from his flight twenty feet off the ground, his features set in stark pain. If there was any doubt about the reason for his actions, they're plain now. Something is hurting him. Something is killing him, and it's not a fall from the rope line.

He lands with shocking ease, proving he's been listening when Bethany instructs me. "What's going on?" he asks Liam.

"There's something you need to see." He nods at Romeo, who stands in the shadows, square-jawed and remote as usual. Dierdre looks like an ice queen, though I suspect there's more to her than she ever shows us. "All of you."

We follow him backstage, none of the others questioning the reason why. It's one thing for me to obey Liam. I do that with complete trust. The others seem to recognize the inherent strength and leadership in him. They respect him in a way that even Josh didn't earn.

The green room is a lounge area for the performers to use before the event. Not the same thing as a dressing room. This has couches and a TV. Depending on the size of the venue, this might be a large, luxurious space or it might be a cramped room. In this theater it's doubling as instrument storage, so we crowd at a scarred wooden table with tubas and timpani.

Liam unfolds a laptop and presses a few keys. "It's going live tomorrow."

I recognize the music from the interview. Images from the tour flash across the screen in artistic array. Liam makes the tape speed up. The video stops on the host's face. Ricky Lightfoot. He's not wearing his signature Hollywood smile. Instead he looks solemn. "This glittering group of men and women represent the future of music and art, full of promise. Darkness lurks beneath the surface. Where did Romeo Perez come from? Was the death of Ambassador Alistair Brooks, the father of violin prodigy Samantha Brooks, really a heart attack? And maybe most disturbing of all, where is the renowned cellist Jessica Kim? She was publicly linked to tenor Harry March only months before her disappearance."

I watch with the same horror I felt as Harry March missed his cue to catch me, as I swung back toward the crowd, clinging to the rope for dear life, as Ricky dissects our pasts. Dierdre comes from a wealthy family that owns a hedge fund. There's speculation of insider trading and illegal activity. Ricky makes a compelling case that Romeo came from a major crime family in El Salvador. It would be almost fantastical, the way he connects grainy pictures of a lost little boy and the mysterious appearance of the dancer in the Cirque du Monde. Plus, there's the fact that he's disturbingly on point with my history. He claims to have spoken to a member of the household staff who said my father had collapsed but was still breathing at the time his private physician arrived.

Bethany's background is without controversy but disturbingly invasive. He has childhood photos of her holding a popsicle and riding a big dog around the yard, where you can see a small but sweet green one-story home in the background. In the next picture it's gutted, the door and window missing, part of the roof caved in, everything still wet from the flood.

My blood runs cold as Ricky moves on to

Jessica Kim.

Liam hits the space bar, and the video freezes on a video of her playing. The cello is cousin to the violin, with a deeper voice and larger size. The musician holds the violin. The cello, with its foot firmly planted on the ground, holds the musician. In the still, Jessica has her arms wrapped around the body, her shoulders draped against the neck in an intimate embrace. Her head bends toward the instrument, as if it's whispering a secret only she can hear.

LIAM

HARRY MARCH CAN'T stop staring at the screen. I recognize the way he looks at Jessica Kim, because it's the same way I must look at Samantha. Devoted to the point of insanity. He looks like a starving man being shown a feast. Is that because he misses his ex-girlfriend? Because he's worried about her disappearance?

Or because he feels guilty for killing her?

I didn't think Harry was a cold-blooded killer. Because I'm one. We can usually recognize our own kind. Like knows like. Then again, it might not have been murder in cold blood. Maybe they got into an argument. He pushed her. She hit her head and bled out. It's a tale as old as fucking time. Whatever happened, we're not leaving this room until I know.

Calmness settles over me. I've tortured men for information. Doesn't matter how much money they're being paid or who indoctrinated them. It's a question of biology. No one can hold out forever. I don't think it will come to that. If I'm right about Harry, if he wants to help Jessica Kim, he'll tell me everything without me pulling out any of the weapons on my person.

"Where is Jessica Kim?"

He flinches. No, this won't take long. "So you can sell it to the tabloids?"

"If you hurt her, you're going to jail. That will be the preferable option. You don't want me to make you disappear the way she disappeared."

"I'd never hurt her," he says, his voice rough. For all the alcohol he's been drinking lately, he looks painfully sober. "I love her."

Love her. Present tense. "Then she's alive?"

"I don't know."

Samantha looks at him with obvious sadness in her brown eyes. It's clear she cares about the asshole, even though he almost dropped her in their first show. "Tell us what you know, Harry. Maybe Liam can help."

He shakes his head, but it's less of a refusal. More like he can't believe this is where life has taken him. "I met her in Tokyo. I had a concert there, and I went out to a bar with some friends. I was drinking and dancing and fucking." He glances at me, his eyes hooded. "Sorry."

"Continue," I say.

"There was this big strip of clubs, everything open late and hopping. And there she was, playing on the street. This world-class talent, on the street with her cello case open for a handful of yen. She was already known by then. She'd done a little performing, but her family had no money so she took her cello out every weekend and played."

Samantha's eyes fill with tears. It's clear this story doesn't have a happy ending. I wish I could have spared her this. I thought about it. It would have been easy to drag Harry March into the room alone. Easy to get the information out of him with force.

But Samantha is a part of this.

Harry holds out his hands, ever the showman. "I stood there watching her play, flirting with her, emptying my pockets into her cello case until she agreed to go for coffee. Which she had to pay for because I already gave her all my cash."

"What happened?" Samantha breathed.

"Her father was a doctor, but he wasn't licensed in Japan. They were refugees from North Korea. Lucky to be alive." His voice breaks. "Lucky to be out of there."

Bethany touches his arm. "I'm so sorry."

"Yeah. So. I learned more about the situation. About the country and how fucking horrible it is, because of what happened to her as a little kid. And I started speaking out. Advocating. Working with a group that helped people escape. Until then, they'd pretty much let her family go. They knew what had happened, because she was semi-famous by then, but they didn't want to piss off Japan. I started donating money, though. Started speaking up. Shaking things up. I had no fucking idea it would put her in danger. I was so stupid."

"You weren't stupid to try and help," Samantha says, tears damp on her cheeks.

"They took her. When she was visiting me in the US. Can you believe it? She was so close in Japan, but they have all kinds of laws and protocols. They took her from the goddamn airport. Herded her onto a private plane before anyone saw that she was being coerced."

"Why the cover-up?" I ask. Sometimes it's the publicity that helps get prisoners released.

"I wanted to tell every goddamn newspaper,

every tabloid. What's the point of being a celebrity if you can't do that? The government officials said that would make it harder to negotiate. There were all these rules, like we can't help you if you don't do what we say. Not that it fucking mattered. They didn't get her back."

"Do you have proof of life?"

Samantha gasps at the question, but I need to know what we're dealing with.

He shakes his head. "The government people had all these plans and documents in the first few months. And then it got quiet. Nothing. No one will talk to me."

"Maybe we can help Jessica Kim." Though maybe not. It's possible she's already dead. Probably she's been tortured. Raped. Things don't sound good for her. I'm not insensitive to that, but my first priority is sitting in this room. "Tell me why you agreed to do the tour. Tell me why you insisted Samantha be part of it."

He bows his head. "I'm sorry."

I slam my fist on the table, making everyone jump. "Tell. Me."

When he looks up at me, he stares into my eyes, pleading for what—understanding? No. I may pity this man and his guilt over Jessica Kim. But I will never feel anything but cold retribution for someone who puts Samantha in harm's way. "The label already had us booked for the tour, but it hadn't been announced yet. I backed out. There was no fucking way I could do it while Jessica was still missing. The government agencies had stopped taking my calls. Someone got in touch with me. Said they could pull strings with the North Korean government if I did the tour, if I asked Samantha Brooks to be part of it."

Everything in me turns cold. "That wasn't all."

"It was supposed to be." He runs a hand through his curly hair, clenching hard enough to make himself flinch. "Then they wanted me to bring her to the Den. Then I had to help someone get into the Grand."

Samantha makes a sound of pain in her throat. "No."

"I'm sorry. That was it. Okay? They wanted me to do more than that, but I told them fucking no. Even if it means—" His voice broke. "Losing Jessica. I couldn't risk you getting hurt so I could save her."

"That's a very convenient decision to make after you'd already let a man with a gun into her dressing room. Why did you believe this person who contacted you?"

"He had a picture of her." Harry reaches into his pocket, and I rest my hand on my gun. If anything other than a photograph appears, there's going to be a bullet between his strawberry blond eyebrows. It's only his phone. He enters his code and opens a file.

A picture appears, a small cot with dingy white sheets. A young woman curled up on her side, dark hair spilling over her face. Bruises darken her wrist. I can see the resemblance. Rage builds in my stomach. To the men who hurt this woman. To Harry March, for endangering Samantha. To the nameless, faceless fucker who enticed him to do it. He's not really a mystery, though. It's her father, with all the right ties to corrupt fucking governments. North Korea wasn't his stomping ground when he was an ambassador but he probably knew a few dirty officials. Like knows like.

"I'll help you get her back. If she's still alive, we'll find her."

Harry looks like he doesn't want to hope. It's happening anyway. "Can you do that?"

"If he says he can, he can," Samantha says, her voice gentle, encouraging. Sympathetic. She isn't going to hold it against March that he could have gotten her killed.

I'm not quite so forgiving. "You're going to give me everything I want. Details on how he contacted you. Access to your phone and email. Your complete cooperation."

Harry stands, swallowing hard. "Anything."

That's when I throw a right hook, catching him across the jaw. I won't break anything, but he's going to need ice on that. He lands in an ungainly sprawl. Bethany lets out a shriek of surprise. Samantha puts her head in her hands.

I shake out my hand. "That's for putting Samantha in danger. Consider yourself lucky. You got off easy. Now let's get to work."

CHAPTER EIGHTEEN

Mahler finished writing Kindertotenlieder, translated "Songs on the Death of Children" a few weeks after his daughter was born. She died years later in childhood.

JOSH

HOTEL BARDOT IS a contemporary hotel taking up the top ten floors of the skyscraper. It's a marked difference from L'Etoile. There are clean lines and slate walls. Miles of crisp white bedding on a dark-wood platform. I'm standing on the roof, where fires dance in rectangular containers and couples lounge in the inky saltwater pool. From here I can see the Grand, though my brother and Samantha are no longer there. I'm not precisely sure where they are at this moment. In the city, probably. My access to North Security's servers has been cut. I'm disowned, apparently. No longer part of the family business. What will I do without an excuse to kill people?

The wind. The water. There is no sound that

doesn't belong, but I feel the shift in the air. He's behind me. "I should shoot you," I say, my tone casual, my palms resting on the iron rail.

"You aren't going to do that," comes the accented, slightly rasping voice. He's been hiding away like a rat in a hole. And Liam? He's the cat—waiting, waiting. "There are too many witnesses."

That makes me smile, though there's no humor in it. Only self-derision. "Do you think I wouldn't go to jail for my brother? Do you think I wouldn't silence the whole fucking floor for him?"

Silence is a pretty word for killing.

"Your loyalty to your brother is admirable. It's a shame he doesn't feel the same way about you."

My brother feels things for me. Guilt, mostly. For not taking enough beatings on my behalf. For not getting us out of there as children. For walking away when he enlisted. The last one? I blamed him for that. It was a cold fucking day when he got on that bus.

The North family doesn't do love. We don't have Christmas and birthdays. We aren't capable of forming ties like ordinary people. Even with Samantha, I'd say it's more obsession than love.

"You want to tell me why you've chosen this

moment to climb out of your fucking hole? You've had six years to get revenge. A little late to the party."

Alistair Brooks joins me at the railing, watching the city. "It may not seem like it, but I do care for my daughter. I'm aware that she was taken care of with Liam North, better than I ever did. That would have been enough for me to let his actions go."

Shock holds me very still. He isn't here to take revenge on Liam?

"Besides, he was only following orders."

So he doesn't know that my brother broke rank. "So walk away. Or better yet, walk right off this building. The world would be better off without you in it."

A gallic shrug. "It's human nature to want to survive. And the things that Samantha might know? I would not survive if they became public. It was safer when he kept her away from the press. When he kept her from performing. I need to find out how much she remembers."

This is about her. It's always been about her. "And if it's nothing?"

"Then I would not harm her. I'm not a monster."

Unfortunately, I'm very familiar with monsters, the kind who will hurt their own children if they believe there is a reason. I want to pretend I don't give a shit about Samantha, but my stomach turns at the thought of her being hurt. "And if she does remember?"

"As I said, it's human nature to want to survive."

A tinkle of laughter comes from behind us. I never thought I'd end up in jail. Is it because I'm too cocky to believe I'd be caught? Or because I just never cared enough to fight for something. Until now.

I care about my brother.

I even care about Samantha, even though I'd rather not.

If I have to shoot someone in front of thirty witnesses, well, that's one way to fucking go. I hope I look good in an orange jumpsuit, because it's going to be a long stay.

My gun is reassuring and solid in my palm.

"Ah ah," he says, motioning toward the ground beneath our feet. A red dot hovers there. A sniper rifle pointed at us. At me. I suppose I could still kill him. Would I get my gun in time? Would I pull the trigger? There's a certain romance to the old-western duel aspect.

Though even if I killed Brooks, his sniper

would kill me.

The man smiles slightly, revealing white teeth that look disturbing set in his ragged face. "You see? Human nature. Even you don't want to die."

Liam wouldn't hesitate. He'd have grabbed the man and launched him over the side if it meant keeping Samantha safe. I guess that's the difference between us. I've never wanted to be the martyr. Even so, I'll do anything for my brother. Until I see another red dot appear—this one on the back of the head of a woman in a white bikini. The word BRIDE is written in glitter across her ass. The man she's cuddling wears black swim shorts that probably say GROOM in a place I can't see. It's an embarrassing wardrobe ensemble, but not worth killing over.

"Really," I say in a low drawl.

Not only one accomplice. Two. If this had been an official North Security operation, we would have been the ones with snipers. We'd have scouted this building eight hours ago. They would have held positions like perfect little GI Joes, pissing into cups if it meant keeping cover.

This isn't an official North Security operation. After basically running the fucking business for years, my brother kicked me out. It would hurt, if I were still capable of feeling pain.

232

CHAPTER NINETEEN

A "monster concert" is an exhilarating show with ten or more
pianos playing at the same time that dates back to the 18th
century in Leipzig.

SAMANTHA

THE NEXT FEW shows on the US tour are tense but uneventful. Harry doesn't get wasted at noon anymore, but he's almost blind with anxiety and grief when he isn't drinking. He does lose some of his charm onstage. Not so much that our reviews suffer. Enough that the press thinks I'm shining even brighter. And I suppose I am becoming more comfortable onstage, able to play with the audience. The more joyful and exaggerated my movements, the more the crowd loves me. I showed up with the ability to play the violin. This? It's a confidence game, and mine's going up. Which is ironic, considering I didn't actually get the gig due to my skill. My father's the reason why Harry March asked for me. It would be a blow to my ego, if it weren't for the increasing fandom that declares me the new star of classical music.

"Listen up," Tracy says, clapping her hands. She stands at the first row of seats while we're lined up onstage. "We've gotten amazing press, but all that's done is increase expectation. Seats are being resold for three times their purchase price. Everyone wants to come see this, and this is the show they'll remember us by."

"No pressure," Bethany murmurs to me, and I snort softly. We've developed a quiet friendship in the raging storm that is the show. She hasn't gotten as much press, but all of us feel the intensity. There are days that start at 6 a.m. for hair and makeup, hours of back-to-back inter-views, rehearsals, and a show—all before we get on a plane for the next city.

The record label makes me a website and social media sites to capitalize on the attention. It's surreal to see people liking and commenting on posts on an Instagram feed I don't even have the login for. There are videos of me on tour, photos of me in costume. The visuals of the Alice in Wonderland theme make for a great feed. There are stylish quotes about music interspersed with shots of lattes I never drank. A line of violin-themed merchandise appears in my stories. Swipe up to get your tote bag! A message from my agent confirms I'm getting a percentage of that. What I do onstage? That's just an act. This, though, feels like a true trip down the rabbit hole. Like I'm in a strange world with wild creatures.

"Harry," Staci says in that singsong, overfriendly way. "We want to see that signature Harry March charm at this show. Let's make all the women swoon, and all the men secretly wish they were gay."

"Right," Harry says, looking up as if to keep himself sane. "Secretly gay. Got it."

The last show in the North American leg of the tour is at Carnegie Hall in New York City. It's a dream come true, salted with the stress of what will happen to Jessica Kim. What will happen to Harry, if she isn't found soon. He looks as if he's ready to break in half.

Tracy frowns, clearly not liking the sarcasm in his tone. "This is why you're the headliner of the tour, Harry. Not that you would know, to look at the social media coverage."

Harry reaches for his belt buckle and starts opening it. "If you want the women to fuck me, maybe I can strip down. Turn this whole thing into a Magic Mike show. Then we can let everyone pretend they give a fuck about music when they actually just want my junk in their face."

I step in front of Harry as if there's an actual bullet heading his way. It's become something of a side job for me to protect him from the harshness of reality. Not that he's ever asked me to do that. If anything he's kind of pissed about it, but then he's pissed about everything lately. And I understand why. That's what makes me want to act as a buffer. "He's going to bring his A game," I say brightly, mirroring Staci's hopeless optimism. He's probably not bringing his A game. Or his B game. Or his C game. We'll be lucky if he actually shows up, especially now that Liam's hinted they're close.

Elijah heads up the team that goes to North Korea. Well, technically I'm never told that's where he goes. Not even in private with Liam. There's the pesky problem of starting an international war to consider. He leaves the room to consult at odd hours, speaking in code words and low tones.

"Don't bother, little violin prodigy." Harry stalks off the stage, throwing us all the middle finger. He would never have done the tour if it hadn't been to get Jessica Kim back. I suppose her return still hinges on this, since he found Liam through me. Though even Liam isn't cold enough to stop helping, even if Harry were to abandon the tour completely.

This tour is going to be headline news one way or another. I'm afraid those words were about more than the record label's PR plans. They're going to come true.

SAMANTHA

I'M SITTING IN one of the boxes at Carnegie Hall, the plush red velvet clinging to my skirt. Rather than being separated by curtains, these little rooms have their own area for hanging coats and a full door that locks. It's more private than most of the boxes I've seen in more modern theaters.

My cheeks flush. It's a good feeling, because the atmosphere on set has been somber ever since Harry's confession. I'm glad he confided in us, even if it was basically coerced by the reality show and Liam's insistence. The door creaks, and I look back to see Liam leaning against the frame. We've been sleeping in the same suite overlooking Times Square, eating from the same breakfast cart, taking the same black car to Carnegie Hall for the past few days. There's been a distance between us. The abandon of the safe house is gone. Funny that it took a break in security to make him lose control. It almost feels worth it to be in danger, if it means seeing the real Liam behind the controlled, serious façade. The Liam that would tear off my panties and ride me until I passed out.

Dim lights cast an expectant glow over the crown molding and dark-wood chairs. The entire building waits for tonight, holding its breath. Liam's green eyes flicker from across the small box. My heart thumps against my ribs. "Nervous?" he asks, his voice low and even.

"Not about the show. I think we have it down by now. The other stuff, though? Yeah. I think Harry's going to lose his mind if we don't hear something soon."

Liam looks out at the stage. "There's news."

My pulse kickstarts into high gear. "There is? Good or bad?"

His gaze meets mine, and I see the answer—both. "Elijah's got her. She's on a plane over the Atlantic Ocean right now. She should be here around midnight."

"Oh my God. We have to tell Harry."

"I already looked for him. He went out. No one knows where."

In New York City? He's a needle in a haystack. At least he'll be back for the performance.

How will he perform knowing she's coming? I don't think he'll be in a state of mind to make women want to fuck him or make men secretly want to be gay, but it doesn't matter. We'll figure out the performance. The important thing is Jessica Kim. "Is she hurt?"

"Yes." He doesn't sugarcoat this for me. I don't want him to, even though it feels like someone's tearing my organs out. I never met the cellist, but she could have been me. Playing on the street for money? At the mercy of dark forces in the world? This was her spot in the show. I replaced her, and part of me feels the connection as strongly as if I felt her pain. "Some of it physical. Most of it mental."

"Does she have a doctor? Is there anything I can do to help?"

"She's had preliminary first aid, but she's going to need a lot more. There's still the issue of secrecy. I want to take her to Kingston. We have the resources to tend to her, and she'll be safe if the government tries to retaliate."

I bite my lip, hoping Harry will agree to that. I'm actually not sure how he's going to take her return. I know he wants her back, but he's spun so far off the rails of normalcy that he can't just snap back, can he? "How is she getting into the

US without a trail?"

"We have some connections with a private airport north of the city."

"She can't stay in Kingston forever, though. What about after?"

"She'll need premium security for some time. Probably forever. The danger's never going away. If she wants to continue playing publicly. Another option would be to assume a new name. A new identity. That would be safer, but she could never play again."

"What do you mean?"

"Playing at that level? It would give her away. There are maybe two people in the world who can rival her. Even regular people understand greatness when they hear it."

To give up playing, though? It would feel like death. "She could try not to—"

"Not to play with incredible skill? I don't think so. Could you?"

No, I can only play the way I play. I don't think it's even possible for me to change it, to sound more ordinary, though it wouldn't satisfy me even if I could. A knot forms in my throat. Her life or her heart. Which one will she choose?

At least she'll have time to recover before facing that decision, although considering what things might have happened to her, that may be a road too long to ever completely walk.

Liam tips his head forward. "I imagine… if he sees her, he may not be able to do the show. I could wait until after to tell him about this."

It may seem frivolous to some people, but this is our career. Our livelihoods. The music that's our soul. This is the way we're able to perform it. Risking the show would harm more than the record label's bottom line. It would harm the reputation of every performer here. Maybe tank an entire career. Trash our life's work. Harry would not care in the moment, but he might care in five years, ten years, if he's not able to get another record deal because of this.

Liam stands there looking strong and implacable. A building that's stood for a hundred years. One that will stand for a hundred more. That's not exactly true, though, is it? It's an illusion. A building can be restored, its pieces replaced, so it looks the same. A person can't be replaced. Liam's work puts him in danger. Being close to me? That makes him a target. If he were in pain, if he needed me, there is nothing that would stop me. No show. No career. Not even music would be enough to hold me back from him. "We have to tell him. It will be up to him what he does."

He hesitates. "There's this phenomenon that can happen when a soldier's lost at sea. He can survive hours, days, even weeks. Using his training and undiluted adrenaline."

My throat clenches, imagining Liam in such a scenario.

"Sometimes when they're rescued, the next day, that's when they die. The body finally relaxes. It stops fighting so hard, and the heart fails."

The heart fails. "Do you think that's what could happen to Jessica Kim?"

A short shake of his head. "I think it could happen to Harry. He's been holding on so long. Sometimes it's the other side that's harder to survive."

I let my hair fall over my face, a black veil. "I feel like a terrible person. Thinking of what happened to Jessica, of how worried Harry's been, and I'm sitting here feeling excited for the performance tonight. How messed up is that?"

He kneels down in front of me, catching my chin with his forefinger. "Not messed up at all. This is a dream come true for so many musicians. A lifetime achievement, and you're only on the cusp of it, Samantha. There's so much left for you."

His green eyes search mine, and I might as well be back in Kingston. Back in the music room practicing for hours while Liam watches me. My cheeks turn hot; I remember the time he spread my legs. The time he made me come while I played Beethoven's 5 Secrets.

"How do you reconcile it?" I ask, but I don't really mean Jessica and Harry. Not only them. I mean the horrible things Liam has seen at war. His own hellish childhood.

"That's what life is about," he says, his eyes darkening to emerald, "Trying to find a moment of happiness in the face of overwhelming human suffering."

"Only a moment?" It makes me think pulling me out of that orphanage wasn't only selfless. It wasn't only a man atoning for his mistake. I give him that moment. That respite from overwhelming human suffering. With my innocence. With my music.

With my body. It makes me want to do it again.

I gave him that much, but it isn't enough. How can it be? He gives me complete devotion. He gives me protection. He books studio time so I can record my song.

"A moment?" His voice turns hoarse. "It's

more than I thought I'd have."

Overwhelming human suffering. It occurs to me that Liam is the walking, talking embodiment of overwhelming human suffering. It defines his life. It shapes his actions. That's why he can't let himself love or be loved. He doesn't know what it means not to suffer. For us to be together? It's giving food to a starving man.

He's been hungry so long all he can manage is a bite. God, I asked him for a hug in that safe house—he gave me sex. I reach out for him now, my palm cupping his face, a good three inches away. He flinches hard enough so that I can't touch him.

God, what if he never really wanted me?

What if he never really loved me?

This whole thing could be about that single night—the guilt he felt over a twelve-year-old girl he didn't even know. How long would he spend atoning for it? My heart already knows the answer: forever. That's not a real relationship. There's no hope of that. "Liam... I think you should leave. After this show, after we go abroad. Don't follow me."

His green eyes turn murky. "You don't mean that."

"I'm dead serious." Even though it will probably kill me. The alternative would kill *him.* How long can he give and give and give, without ever getting anything in return? How long can he bear the burdens of the world without ever leaning on anyone?

I left his house looking for independence. Instead I discovered that my ties are too strong to be severed. I left looking for freedom. Instead I found knowledge. Like a kaleidoscope coming into focus—he's more clear to me now than he has ever been.

It took leaving Liam to find him.

He's breathing in hard swallows. "Samantha."

Heat stings my eyes. This was always going to happen. It was only a question of when. "You've been pushing me away for a year. You've been keeping me at a distance since we met in that orphanage. Now I'm finally ready to accept your decision."

He looks so impossibly handsome standing in a white button-down and black slacks. He prefers cargo pants and a T-shirt, but he always dresses nice for the performances. The suit fits him as easily as his combat gear. Even now, his ocean-green eyes turbulent, he looks completely in control. "I love you. You know that?"

"Do you?" I have to fight back the rise of

tears, the ache in my throat. "Or do you love taking care of me? Do you love breaking yourself into pieces for me?"

Surprise moves over his face. Followed by guilt. "No."

A rough laugh escapes me. "You couldn't even bring yourself to hug me without also fucking me. I don't know if you're capable of experiencing affection that doesn't end in you feeling terrible for taking advantage of me."

"You want me to forget who you are to me?"

I stood up to Harry and to the record label. I even stood up to my father. It was only a matter of time before I stood up to Liam. He had to be last—and the most heartbreaking. A tear slips between my lashes, pooling against my cheek. "I want you to see me for who I am now. You're determined to think I'm helpless. I'm still twelve years old and orphaned to you, so maybe it is wrong for you to fuck me, Liam. If you can't treat me like a woman then you don't deserve to keep me. You don't get to be the hero and the villain."

His voice comes out hoarse. "I don't want to lose you."

"No." Bitterness tightens my throat. "You don't. But that's not enough." Isn't that what Ocha said about choice? *It has not been my experience that it matters much, Ms. Brooks. Can a violin choose to be a piano? We are what we are.*

"What will it take—some kind of sacrifice?" He sounds angry about it.

"You'd love that, wouldn't you? That would be just the thing for you. The martyr. The savior. I don't want you to hurt for me, Liam. Can't you see that? I don't want to hurt for you. That isn't how love should be."

He swallows. "It's the only way I know how."

"Me too." A sob overtakes me then. If Alice represents curiosity and innocence, then the Queen of Hearts is pained feminine knowledge. They aren't two separate people. They're two sides of the same coin. One hopeful, one desolate. One searching out friends. One alone.

He steps forward as if to embrace me.

I hold out my hand to ward him away.

When did he become the thing I need protection from? I love him, but it does hurt—like kneeling on jagged rocks. It almost feels worse to finally stand up. That's the way we learned to love. The pattern needs to break.

He grew up protecting his brothers and keeping enough emotional distance that he could walk away. I grew up desperately trying to please men who would never really be pleased. My violin became the way I proved my worth. It became the way I fought for them to love me.

That's the irony of this concerto.

The stage was both my freedom and my cage.

I walk away with my eyesight shimmering and unclear, clinging to the banister and tripping gracelessly down the stairs of Carnegie Hall, this place that held so many dreams. I leave him behind in the private box. Watching. He isn't part of this performance any longer. He isn't part of me.

CHAPTER TWENTY

Stalin disliked the work of composer Shostakovich. Shortly before the premiere of his new symphony, a Soviet official attended a rehearsal. The work was withdrawn by Shostakovich. It did not premiere until after Stalin's death, some 25 years after the work was composed.

SAMANTHA

B Y THE TIME seven o'clock rolls around, I'm not worried about telling Harry.

I'm worried about where he is.

Even drunk and unruly and belligerent, he never missed a curtain call completely. As the minutes count down, it seems like that's what's happening. It makes me wonder if he got into some real trouble. Anything could happen in New York City. What if he ended up in jail? Or what if he's in some hospital right now? They wouldn't know who to contact.

Two minutes to showtime. One.

The curtain doesn't always rise on time. It depends on the people working the local venue and the set designers. It depends on whether we're squeezing into our costumes at the last minute. Tonight seemed to stretch out to infinity. I had a billion years to put on my blue silk and white lace.

The white-haired man approaches me. "Where is he?"

I swallow hard. "I have no idea. He didn't tell me anything."

"You're the one fucking him. You're telling me you can't even hold his attention for three months?"

Shock tightens my throat. "Do you honestly believe your own publicity stunts? We never had that kind of relationship. And you have no right to speak to me that way."

"I have every right. The money we've put into this tour… it's my reputation on the line with the label, all because a bunch of spoiled kids don't know how to sing and dance."

Before I have a chance to reply, his face twists into an array of pain. Liam appears behind him. Some kind of fancy hold on his arm. That explains the agonized sound he's making. "Let go of him," I say, raising my chin so Liam knows I'm serious about this.

Liam's green eyes narrow. He wants to make the man hurt more. I won't be swayed. He's here to protect me from real danger, not fighting a professional battle.

He steps aside.

"We're all worried about Harry," I say, my voice soft but unmistakably serious. "So I'll let your words slide. If you ever speak to me or any of the other performers like that again, I'll go to the label and tell them about your disrespect. It's not your money invested in the tour; it's theirs, and if they want us to stick around to sing and dance, they'll be willing to fire you."

The man stomps away. Liam raises his eyebrows. "That was sexy."

I huff an exasperated laugh. "You do realize I've been going through hair and makeup for hours every other night, and this is when you decide to compliment me?"

His emerald eyes flash. "Do you doubt that I find you beautiful?"

My cheeks heat, because I can't really doubt it. Not when his body becomes hard whenever we're in the same room. Not when he shivers in my arms, this strong man made weak from my touch.

Bethany and I exchange a look. "I tried his cell," she says. "It's going straight to voicemail. I left a message. And texted him. And emailed, but

I don't think it's going to matter."

My lips tighten. "Can Romeo do the choreography?"

"Of course. He can't sing though. I mean he *really* can't sing."

"We're going to skip that part. We'll have the orchestra do an instrumental melody. The audience doesn't know it's supposed to be Harry's part. With any luck he'll stroll in a few minutes after we start."

A murmur of concern comes through the curtain. By the time I confer with the conductor, who handles the impromptu change like a pro, we're thirty minutes past the curtain opening. I stumble out through the back entrance, looking lost and confused as I chase an imaginary rabbit down the red carpet. Romeo performs the choreography flawlessly, partnering me with more skill and confidence than Harry could. In unspoken agreement we draw out the flourishes at every step.

Every venue has its own quirks. Some of them are more like stadiums, with high-tech sound and lighting equipment—their acoustics more appropriate for a big bass rock concert. Carnegie Hall is an intimate setting. I feel the energy of the audience immediately, their anticipation. The building was made for the clear, high strains of the violin. When I pick up my violin and play Mendelssohn, I can feel it move through the air on the backs of a thousand performances before this one. Doing this many performances in a row, I know when I have the audience, when they're spellbound, when my playing is connecting— that's what's happening tonight. Despite the frantic beginning, or maybe because of it, I sink deep into the song. The violin sings in my arms, proud to be part of this performance heritage.

When I get backstage, I'm breathing hard, exhilarated and flushed.

Bethany and Romeo are doing their routine early in the show, but it soon won't be possible to hide the fact that Harry's missing. I don't know what the protocol is—don't plays usually have an understudy? This isn't a play, though. It's a concert.

We should have cancelled, I realize. Don't the label reps decide that?

Bethany and Romeo's routine comes to a crescendo.

"What did I miss?" The low voice comes behind me, and I whirl to see Harry standing there, his purple suit rumpled, his damp hair more red than blond. He doesn't seem drunk, which is about the nicest thing I can say about him. His eyes are wild, out of control. "Aw, you started without me."

"Oh my God," I say, feeling sick to my stomach. It's like realizing you're standing onstage naked. That would almost be easier. At least we could pretend it was for sex appeal. This is worse. We're holding a concert in the most important venue in the United States without our headliner.

He smiles. "Don't worry, little violinist. You'll still have your career."

I'm not entirely sure that's true. Not if the label reps tell the higher-ups and executives that I was actually sleeping with Harry March. It doesn't matter now. I'm more concerned with the unhinged light in his eyes as he steps onto the stage. I'm tugging at his arm, trying to stop him. "Someone help me," I say, but he pulls both of us into the spotlight.

That casual stroll. That signature smile. They don't have any idea how much pain it hides. Although they're about to find out. He snags the microphone from a stand. "Good evening, New York City," he says with a showman's wave of his arm.

There's a smattering of responses. Smiles in the audience. Some uncertain looks. This is clearly more impromptu than they were expecting, but it's still probably part of the routine, right? He's going to dazzle them. That's what they got dressed up for tonight—to be dazzled.

"You look so beautiful tonight. So fucking handsome. Does that make you want to be secretly gay, New York City? Does that make you want to jizz your suit pants?"

"Oh my God," I whisper. I'm caught like a fish on a string, unable to stand this horrible limelight, unable to scamper offstage where I could hide.

"I'm told I'm supposed to make you want to fuck me, but I don't know about that. See, I don't want to fuck any of you. Don't I get a say in this? What about my right to consent in the fuckability games?"

It's not my most dignified moment—I lunge for the mic in his hand. He's way taller than me. He yanks it out of my grasp, and I wobble on my white lace flats. If only I had a real cup of crazy tea that I could drink and become twenty feet tall. I'd be able to grab the microphone away. Or maybe just stomp Harry into oblivion—yes, that's what I'd do. Anything but hop around uselessly while Harry says, "Let's talk about North Korea, ladies and gentlemen. I've been told I can't talk about it. It's not polite to talk about torture, when all you really want to do is imagine fucking me."

Then I actually do manage to snatch the microphone away from him, but it's not because I magically became taller. It's because his arms fall to his sides. His gaze is trained on the door that leads backstage, partially obscured from the audience by the pretend forest foliage. A girl stands in the doorway, eyes wide, skin pale, hair a wild black mane.

Harry goes to her on unsteady legs. His smooth gait completely destroyed. He doesn't even make it all the way to her. His knees fold. He lands at her feet, kneeling, pressing his face to her middle. His shoulders are shaking in voiceless sobs.

Her eyes close on a sigh of aching relief.

It's the most emotional thing I've ever seen, and I'm standing in front of a thousand people. Bethany's eyes are wide, her lips parted in shock. The label reps are there, looking horrified. No one is moving—not in the audience, not backstage. They're waiting for me to do something, to decide something.

I'm watching Harry and Jessica like they're unlocking something inside me. And they are—a memory. *Remember this, Samantha. It's important.*

You can do that for Daddy. The opening notes of my composition came from sheet music he put in front of me.

It wasn't something we shared widely, your memory. You could play music. That was enough of a marvel for the world. They didn't know that you could also memorize ten sheets of music at a glance.

It was bad enough to realize my father used my violin case. Now I realize he may have used more than that—he may have used *me*. My brain, memorizing sheets of paper. They didn't even have to carry anything. Only me and a violin, ready to recite back whatever they gave me. The notes underneath the composition. They mean something.

Liam appears, looking furious. He wants to charge the stage for me; I can see it in his eyes. He wants to put his body between me and the audience, as if their inquisitive eyes are bullets he can protect me from. As if the explosion of my career is an IED he can shield me from. I give a short shake of my head. I can't lean on him anymore. I can't take and take and take, knowing he won't let me give anything back. That isn't a relationship. That isn't love. Humiliation heats my skin. Blood pounds through my veins. This is my battle.

CHAPTER TWENTY-ONE

*Italian violinist Giuseppe Tartini had a dream where he met
the devil, who played him the most beautiful and striking
sonata he'd ever heard. He wrote it down immediately
upon waking.*

LIAM

"THIS ISN'T HOW the show is supposed to
go," she murmurs into the microphone.

Nervous laughter answers her from the velvet
seats. It's a conditioned social response to
awkward situations. Some of them are still hoping
this is part of the show, that they'll launch into a
song that explains everything.

She's so impossibly brave standing there on
that stage, unwilling to run away, facing what
must be any musician's greatest fear. I can't
imagine this has happened too often, the
complete and public breakdown of a show. I
expect her to apologize, in a way that's sincere and
brief, and then leave the stage. There will
probably be outrage. Confusion.

She doesn't leave the stage.

"I've been thinking about… well, about Alice." She looks down at herself with a little hand wave, showing off her costume. It's probably wrong to think about tearing the silk from her lithe body. I never really stop being wrong in that way. "Some people say that Alice is a feminist text because she has curiosity and action. Because she changes her own destiny. Other people say that it's not feminist, because there are all these males around, the cat and the Mad Hatter, even the white rabbit, pulling her this way and that. But I think, how crazy is that? To say that a woman can't be strong if there are men pushing and pulling her. It would mean that no woman is strong. That's the world we live in. Then again, it isn't really a story about a woman, is it? It's a story about a little girl. It's a story about growing up. The Queen of Hearts is the villain of the story. The irrational woman. The angry woman. The woman so tired of being made small and large by men that she becomes a monarch to rule them all. They are not enemies, Alice and the Queen. They are two sides of the same coin. Innocence and awareness. The child and the woman. They are all of us."

She crosses the stage to where her violin waits.

This is the part of the evening where she'd be playing the Philip Glass Violin Concerto 1. It's a piece that never fails to make you *feel* which in musical terms probably means it's great. For a soldier who's learned to make himself numb… less great.

"So I've been thinking about Alice," she says, her voice almost like a lullaby. I'm soothed by her. I think the audience is, too. "And I want to play you a song I wrote."

My breath catches. Her composition. It was one thing to play it in the private sound booth, knowing that I would not show it to anyone without her consent. She could have uploaded it somewhere. Contracted with a label for distribution. She could have done any of those things in a methodical way. This is not methodical. It's impulsive and sweet, as Harry clutches Jessica Kim to his chest behind me.

Her bow touches the strings, and I'm transported. To war zones and deep wells. Transported to a Russian orphanage where a little girl watched a stranger with wide eyes. It's a song about loss, and it fills the theater as beautifully as any one of the great composers. She's taking her place, her rightful place, and judging from the looks on her audience's faces, they know it. This is history.

Most of the audience watches with rapt attention. An older gentleman tilts his head back and closes his eyes, letting the strains wash over him. A few people pull out their phones, even though it's prohibited. This will end up on the internet no matter what.

I'm scanning the rows of people, some old, some young. Every race and culture is represented in this theater. Every hope and dream. That's when I see him.

Alistair Brooks. He's sitting in the fifth row, almost at the end.

Samantha told me once that when she plays the fast notes, she has to slow down. It's the only way to get it right. In her mind there's all the time in the world. Otherwise her fingers trip over themselves. That's how it is during a firefight. And that's what this is about to become—a firefight. Everything slows down.

Brooks reaches into his coat, his expression regretful.

The flash of something silver.

I take a step onto the stage, making myself the bigger target. He wants to use her as bait to kill me—he can have me. He can have his revenge.

If I don't manage to shoot him first.

Pale brown eyes flick over to me. His weapon

still points at Samantha. *Fuck*. What's wrong? Why isn't he trying to kill me? Realization lands like a spray of shrapnel. He isn't after me. This isn't revenge for the assassination. For some reason he's going to shoot her.

Why? It doesn't matter now. The only thing that matters is stopping him.

The notes roll over me like baptismal water, cleansing me of the sin I'm about to commit. He's moving to stand, and I'm already crossing the stage. Time moves at a snail's pace. The thud of my boots on the parquet floor. The last note rising over me. The fall of the bow at her side.

The actual mechanics of the gun aren't even thought. They're habit. An imaginary target appears on his forehead. *Direct hit.* Screams erupt in the theater. There are a thousand witnesses. Phones already recording. I don't mind killing someone. I don't even mind prison if it means keeping Samantha safe. The problem is we had the motive all wrong.

Samantha's gaze whips to mine. Fear. Is she afraid of me?

That's when I see the red dot on her white lace bodice. Terror clamps my chest. There's someone else in the theater. My lungs burn. She's standing there in her blue silk costume, her bow and violin her only shield. I'm running toward her, terrified I won't reach her.

I push her offstage in the opposite direction. Away from Harry March and Jessica Kim. Away from the label reps. Away from her entire future.

Isn't that what I told her? I warned her.

Being with me cost her everything. Her career, her freedom.

Whether she wants this or not, I'm going to keep her safe. Except she doesn't seem safe. She's crying. Her hands grasp my chest, tugging at my shirt. Blood.

There's blood on her hands. I stare at it, un-comprehending. Was she hit? Horror is a cold fist around my heart. I grasp her arms, half-dragging her off the stage, half-falling on her. "Help me," she cries. "Someone help me." *I'm trying.* Everything feels heavy. My arms, my legs. My eyelids. I've been shot. The realization rises like freezing water, forming a layer of ice above me. My training provides a helpful word: shock. That's the reason I don't feel any pain.

I'm shot, which means there's no one to pro-tect Samantha.

The building tilts. Shouts. Screams. More bullets. *No.*

She pulls me off the stage, which shouldn't be

possible with how much bigger I am. It's all those hours practicing, making her strong. And pure adrenaline. She's gasping and crying, telling me everything's going to be okay.

Then Bethany and Romeo are there, helping to pull me backstage. I must be farther gone than I realized. Did the bullet pierce my heart? My body isn't responding. It's a soldier who's gone AWOL—no longer under my command. Am I going to die in Carnegie Hall? It would be fitting after everything I've done.

"What are we going to do?" Bethany's asking. Her voice sounds far away as if she's speaking from underwater. "It's chaos out there. People are climbing the stage. Someone *jumped* off the mezzanine. I don't know if he's okay—"

"People are getting trampled on the stairs. We can't go that way." Romeo's voice. He sounds grim, but not surprised. That's in keeping with his origins. He knows violence.

Samantha sounds shaky but resolute. "I called someone. Liam needs medical attention, and we don't have time for theater security or NYPD to get us out."

Who did she call? I already know.

"He's here," she says.

The three of them work together to drag me

through a fire escape. Bethany's got the violin tucked under her arm—good. That's good. Samantha would be hurt if it got damaged. We land in a damp alley. Streetlights bounce off bricks. Stars span thousands of miles.

I'm going to black out. Not before I make sure Samantha is safe.

If it's the last fucking thing I do…

Sure enough, Josh appears at my side. Cool green eyes take us in. He doesn't even look ruffled by the three of us smeared in blood. "Put him in the trunk. He won't mind."

Samantha gasps. "What is wrong with you? He's sitting in the front."

"Half dead and he still gets shotgun," Josh mutters, but he takes the weight of me as we limp around the back of the black Lincoln. The world has narrowed to a pinpoint. I'm two seconds from passing out. There are reserves somewhere. I find them.

In a millisecond I have Josh pushed against the side of the car, my breathing wild, my arm across his neck. We were in this position in Tanglewood not long ago. Everything's changed now. "Did you know? Did you help him?"

Pain flashes through his eyes. "Did I know he had backing? Yeah, he paid me a little visit. Did I know he was going to be here tonight? No, and I didn't fucking help him."

There's more relief than I want to admit. My brother. He's my brother. I didn't want to think he betrayed me. "Keep her alive. Keep her alive or I'll kill you."

He swallows against my arm. "I understand the priority. Don't worry. No one will touch her while you're unconscious. Got it? Now maybe stop bleeding all over me."

I'm not sure what happens next. I probably keep bleeding, but I'm no longer aware of it. The world gets smaller and smaller, until it goes completely dark.

SAMANTHA

SIRENS BOUNCE OFF the pavement around us. Lights flash—red and blue, red and blue. They're heading in the opposite direction, toward Seventh Avenue, to Carnegie Hall. The audience, the other performers. They need help. We need help. Romeo and Bethany are crammed into the back with me, the violin across our laps, while Liam's passed out in the passenger seat.

A hospital. We need to go to a hospital.

The words sound like they come from someone else. Josh ignores me, driving us to a part of New York City I don't recognize. The buildings shrink down and huddle together. Unblinking windows stare us down. The space between buildings looks too small to fit a car, but we pull through them, a few inches to spare on either side.

"Where are we?" I ask, my teeth chattering. My whole body feels cold and unhinged, as if it's coming apart the farther away we get from Carnegie Hall.

"Somewhere they don't worry too much about people showing up shot and bleeding, but I'd still rather not advertise our location. Help me get him upstairs."

It takes forty-five minutes for a surgeon to arrive. At least I assume he's a surgeon. He removes the bullet while Romeo assists. Apparently he has medical training, because he knows his way around an IV. I don't bother asking how Josh has an underground doctor on speed dial. He wouldn't tell me, and I'm not sure I care as long as Liam's alive.

I breathe every minute of doubt, every second of grief…

It takes two days for the numbness to sink into my skin. Two days of barely sleeping on a ratty couch in the bedroom while Josh takes the floor. We send Bethany back to Cirque du Monde with Romeo once the panic dies down. The tour is on indefinite hiatus, seeing as pretty much all the performers deserted.

Two days of burning fear before the ice builds around me. It's welcome, the lack of feeling. Especially when Josh enters the room carrying a large black box. He flips it open. Empty. Everything inside me tightens.

"For the violin," Josh says, his green eyes shuttered.

It's been a part of me for as long as I can remember. Like a limb. No, more important than that. My heart. He wants to take it from me? There won't be anything left.

"Until when?" I ask, my voice trembling only slightly. As if I don't know the answer. As if I'm Cindy Lou, entrusting her Christmas tree to the Grinch.

"Until we figure out what your memory unlocks."

Only a few days ago I considered how Jessica Kim would feel if she had to give up playing the cello to stay alive. Now that's the situation I'm in. My father wasn't after Liam for revenge. He was pointing the gun at me. Me. Sharp pain lances my heart. He wasn't ever a wonderful father, but this?

I don't think I'll ever get over it. I don't think I can really accept it. No matter how old I get, year after year, there will always be a little girl inside me, wide-eyed and bewildered as her father tried to kill her.

Josh's eyes are darker green than Liam's, but they still remind me of him. Brothers, even though they were fighting at the end. "As long as you keep performing, you're a target. Which means he is, too."

I stroke the gleaming wood of my violin. A Stradivarius worth millions of dollars, shut away in the dark with no one to play. It feels like a crime. There's a shadow of blood on the neck; it really did experience violence.

My throat swallows convulsively. "Then I won't play it."

A raised eyebrow. "You couldn't stop yourself."

He's probably right. After playing every day, I can't quit cold turkey. I can't imagine a world without music. What do people do during those hours between waking and sleeping? Josh pulls my hands away from the violin case, the gentle plucking of flower petals from the stem. Just as well. I don't think I could have physically done it myself. He places the violin in a large black box, the kind that might hold machine guns or explosives.

That's what the violin has become—a weapon.

I press my hand against the cold, marbled plastic of the box. It feels like a heartbeat inside, faint and dying. Though it's probably just the pulse from my hand. "What if it takes months? What if it takes years? I'm not sure I can survive that."

"A bullet lodged two inches from his aorta, Samantha. He almost didn't survive that."

My stomach turns over. So close. So close to losing him. "I'm sorry," I whisper.

"You should be. He never would have dropped his guard if it weren't for you." His expression turns hard. "If it makes you feel any better, it's probably a relief for him. He's been wanting to die to save someone for as long as I've known him."

"Stop it," I say, even though the words echo what I said in the box seats.

What will it take—some kind of sacrifice?

You'd love that, wouldn't you? That would be just the thing for you. The martyr. The savior. I don't want you to hurt for me, Liam.

It doesn't matter what I wanted. That's what

happened.

Josh picks up the black box. "Don't beat yourself up. You got him off the stage and out of the theater. He's alive because of you. I'd just like to keep it that way."

I cross the apartment to the bedroom, where a pale and unnaturally still version of Liam lies beneath the blankets. Miles of bandages cover his chest. Two days of growth shade his jaw. He still looks vibrant and strong. Liters of blood loss and near death hasn't changed that. I half-expect him to go run ten miles or do five hundred push-ups.

Instead he's breathing, breathing, breathing. That's the miracle.

Josh mutters something under his breath about martyrs deserving each other and leaves the room, taking my violin with him. The metal door closes behind him with a slam, and I flinch. Chaos. Screaming. Liam heavy in my arms. Memories assault me in fragments before retreating to their shadows.

A bowl of cool water sits beside the bed. I pick up the washcloth and drench it, before dampening Liam's jaw, his lips, his neck. The part of his shoulder that isn't bandaged. He's hot to the touch. His body's fighting infection, the doctor said. We have medicines, but that doesn't stop me from doing what I can. From touching my fingertips to his pulse to reassure myself he's alive. In the end it was an easy choice—Liam or my violin. I choose him. He spent six years protecting me. It's my turn to protect him.

"When are you going to wake up?" I whisper. There's no answer from the bed. Two hundred and twenty pounds of solid, muscled silence. "Josh says we need to leave the country. That whoever was funding my father—it isn't some faraway corrupt government. It's this one. He doesn't know who we can trust."

I touch my fingers to the back of his hand, trace the tendons and muscles and calluses that form him. Then I slip underneath so we're holding hands. It's a little intimate. A little wrong to make him give me affection in sleep that he never would waking. It would have to be about sex or guilt.

In this moment I steal comfort.

"'That's simple,'" I say in a low pretend-Liam voice. "'Don't trust anyone.'"

He doesn't laugh at my sad joke.

There's probably music for this moment, but I don't hear it—not even in my head. That organ has been ripped away. "Hey," I tell him, my voice wobbly. "You're going to get better. You're going to hate it, being weak for even two seconds. I'm going to help you. You don't have a choice, okay? So don't even argue."

Tears blur my vision. I'm crying hard enough that I almost can't see the sliver of malachite where he's opened his eyes. Joy and perpetual fear clog my throat. "Liam?"

He makes a sound—almost a growl, like an animal. It isn't a word, but it communicates everything. His anguish. His regret. His need. He tightens his hand on mine, holding it back. This is too sweet of a gesture for him to tolerate, but he does. As if I've tamed him.

When I was twelve years old, he saved me, and I have belonged to him ever since. The sudden impact of a bullet, the staggering weight of him, the frantic surge of adrenaline that helped me pull him off the stage.

Maybe I needed to save him back for him to belong to me, too.

Maybe he's finally mine.

The End

Thank you so much for reading CONCERTO. I hope you love the deep emotion and sensuality of Liam and Samantha's story! The final book in the trilogy, SONATA, is out available for you to read now!

Who is Samantha Brooks without her violin? Fear lives in the silent spaces. Love does, too. There's a battle being waged in her heart, and Liam North is determined to win. He'll use every weapon in his arsenal. His body. His heart. Except the spotlight puts her in the crosshairs of dangerous men.

Samantha fights to compose her own ending, even as the final notes rise to a heartbreaking crescendo.

SONATA is available now on all book retailers!

Ready for more Tanglewood? The sexy virgin auction book THE PAWN with Gabriel and Avery is FREE on all retailers! *There's one way to save our house, one thing I have left of value—my body.* You can find THE PAWN on Amazon, Barnes & Noble, Apple Books, and Kobo now!

And you can read Hugo and Bea's story right now! Find out what happens when a seductive and jaded male escort shows up at the penthouse of an innocent heiress…

> "A sensual feast! Escort is extraordinary—delicious, passionate, dreamily sexy and utterly romantic! One of my favorite books of the year and I will be recommending it to everyone!"
>
> —#1 NYT Bestselling author Lauren Blakely

Turn the page for an excerpt from The Pawn…

Excerpt from The Pawn

WIND WHIPS AROUND my ankles, flapping the bottom of my black trench coat. Beads of moisture form on my eyelashes. In the short walk from the cab to the stoop, my skin has slicked with humidity left by the rain.

Carved vines and ivy leaves decorate the ornate wooden door.

I have some knowledge of antique pieces, but I can't imagine the price tag on this one—especially exposed to the elements and the whims of vandals. I suppose even criminals know enough to leave the Den alone.

Officially the Den is a gentlemen's club, the old-world kind with cigars and private invitations. Unofficially it's a collection of the most powerful men in Tanglewood. Dangerous men. Criminals, even if they wear a suit while breaking the law.

A heavy brass knocker in the shape of a fierce lion warns away any visitors. I'm desperate enough to ignore that warning. My heart thuds in my chest and expands out, pulsing in my fingers, my toes. Blood rushes through my ears, drowning out the whoosh of traffic behind me.

I grasp the thick ring and knock—once, twice.

Part of me fears what will happen to me behind that door. A bigger part of me is afraid the door won't open at all. I can't see any cameras set into the concrete enclave, but they have to be watching. Will they recognize me? I'm not sure it would help if they did. Probably best that they see only a desperate girl, because that's all I am now.

The softest scrape comes from the door. Then it opens.

I'm struck by his eyes, a deep amber color— like expensive brandy and almost translucent. My breath catches in my throat, lips frozen against words like *please* and *help.* Instinctively I know they won't work; this isn't a man given to mercy. The tailored cut of his shirt, its sleeves carelessly rolled up, tells me he'll extract a price. One I can't afford to pay.

There should have been a servant, I thought. A butler. Isn't that what fancy gentlemen's clubs have? Or maybe some kind of a security guard. Even our house had a housekeeper answer the door—at least, before. Before we fell from grace.

Before my world fell apart.

The man makes no move to speak, to invite me in or turn me away. Instead he stares at me with vague curiosity, with a trace of pity, the way one might watch an animal in the zoo. That might be how the whole world looks to these men, who have more money than God, more power than the president.

That might be how I looked at the world, before.

My throat feels tight, as if my body fights this move, even while my mind knows it's the only option. "I need to speak with Damon Scott."

Scott is the most notorious loan shark in the city. He deals with large sums of money, and nothing less will get me through this. We have been introduced, and he left polite society by the time I was old enough to attend events regularly. There were whispers, even then, about the young man with ambition. Back then he had ties to the underworld—and now he's its king.

One thick eyebrow rises. "What do you want with him?"

A sense of familiarity fills the space between us even though I know we haven't met. This man is a stranger, but he looks at me as if he wants to know me. He looks at me as if he already does. There's an intensity to his eyes when they sweep over my face, as firm and as telling as a touch.

"I need..." My heart thuds as I think about all the things I need—a rewind button. One person in the city who doesn't hate me by name alone. "I need a loan."

He gives me a slow perusal, from the nervous slide of my tongue along my lips to the high neckline of my clothes. I tried to dress professionally—a black cowl-necked sweater and pencil skirt. His strange amber gaze unbuttons my coat, pulls away the expensive cotton, tears off the fabric of my bra and panties. He sees right through me, and I shiver as a ripple of awareness runs over my skin.

I've met a million men in my life. Shaken hands. Smiled. I've never felt as seen through as I do right now. Never felt like someone has turned me inside out, every dark secret exposed to the harsh light. He sees my weaknesses, and from the cruel set of his mouth, he likes them.

His lids lower. "And what do you have for collateral?"

Nothing except my word. That wouldn't be worth anything if he knew my name. I swallow past the lump in my throat. "I don't know."

Nothing.

He takes a step forward, and suddenly I'm

crowded against the brick wall beside the door, his large body blocking out the warm light from inside. He feels like a furnace in front of me, the heat of him in sharp contrast to the cold brick at my back. "What's your name, girl?"

The word *girl* is a slap in the face. I force myself not to flinch, but it's hard. Everything about him overwhelms me—his size, his low voice. "I'll tell Mr. Scott my name."

In the shadowed space between us, his smile spreads, white and taunting. The pleasure that lights his strange yellow eyes is almost sensual, as if I caressed him. "You'll have to get past me."

My heart thuds. He likes that I'm challenging him, and God, that's even worse. What if I've already failed? I'm free-falling, tumbling, turning over without a single hope to anchor me. Where will I go if he turns me away? What will happen to my father?

"Let me go," I whisper, but my hope fades fast.

His eyes flash with warning. "Little Avery James, all grown up."

A small gasp resounds in the space between us. He already knows my name. That means he knows who my father is. He knows what he's done. Denials rush to my throat, pleas for understanding. The hard set of his eyes, the broad strength of his shoulders tells me I won't find any mercy here.

I square my shoulders. I'm desperate but not broken. "If you know my name, you know I have friends in high places. Connections. A history in this city. That has to be worth something. That's my collateral."

Those connections might not even take my call, but I have to try something. I don't know if it will be enough for a loan or even to get me through the door. Even so, a faint feeling of family pride rushes over my skin. Even if he turns me away, I'll hold my head high.

Golden eyes study me. Something about the way he said *little Avery James* felt familiar, but I've never seen this man. At least I don't think we've met. Something about the otherworldly glow of those eyes whispers to me, like a melody I've heard before.

On his driver's license it probably says something mundane, like brown. But that word can never encompass the way his eyes seem almost luminous, orbs of amber that hold the secrets of the universe. *Brown* can never describe the deep golden hue of them, the indelible opulence in his fierce gaze.

"Follow me," he says.

Relief courses through me, flooding numb limbs, waking me up enough that I wonder what I'm doing here. These aren't men, they're animals. They're predators, and I'm prey. Why would I willingly walk inside?

What other choice do I have?

I step over the veined marble threshold.

The man closes the door behind me, shutting out the rain and the traffic, the entire city disappeared in one soft turn of the lock. Without another word he walks down the hall, deeper into the shadows. I hurry to follow him, my chin held high, shoulders back, for all the world as if I were an invited guest. Is this how the gazelle feels when she runs over the plains, a study in grace, poised for her slaughter?

The entire world goes black behind the staircase, only breath, only bodies in the dark. Then he opens another thick wooden door, revealing a dimly lit room of cherrywood and cut crystal, of leather and smoke. Barely I see dark eyes, dark suits. Dark men.

I have the sudden urge to hide behind the man with the golden eyes. He's wide and tall, with hands that could wrap around my waist. He's a giant of a man, rough-hewn and hard as stone.

Except he's not here to protect me.

He could be the most dangerous of all.

✧   ✧   ✧

The price of survival…

Gabriel Miller swept into my life like a storm. He tore down my father with cold retribution, leaving him penniless in a hospital bed. I quit my private all-girl's college to take care of the only family I have left.

There's one way to save our house, one thing I have left of value.

My virginity.

A forbidden auction…

Gabriel appears at every turn. He seems to take pleasure in watching me fall. Other times he's the only kindness in a brutal underworld.

Except he's playing a deeper game than I know. Every move brings us together, every secret rips us apart. And when the final piece is played, only one of us can be left standing.

"Skye Warren's THE PAWN is a triumph of intrigue, angst, and sensual drama. I was clenching everything. Gabriel and Avery sucked me in from the first few paragraphs

and never let go."

Want to read more? The Pawn is available on Amazon, iBooks, Barnes & Noble, and other book retailers!

BOOKS BY SKYE WARREN

Endgame trilogy & more books in Tanglewood

The Pawn

The Knight

The Castle

The King

The Queen

Escort

Survival of the Richest

The Evolution of Man

A Modern Fairy Tale Duet

Beauty and the Professor

Falling for the Beast

Chicago Underground series

Rough

Hard

Fierce

Wild

Dirty

Secret

Sweet

Deep

Stripped series

Tough Love

Love the Way You Lie

Better When It Hurts

Even Better

Pretty When You Cry

Caught for Christmas

Hold You Against Me

To the Ends of the Earth

For a complete listing of Skye Warren books, visit

www.skyewarren.com/books

About the Author

Skye Warren is the New York Times bestselling author of dangerous romance such as the Endgame trilogy. Her books have been featured in Jezebel, Buzzfeed, USA Today Happily Ever After, Glamour, and Elle Magazine. She makes her home in Texas with her loving family, sweet dogs, and evil cat.

Sign up for Skye's newsletter:
www.skyewarren.com/newsletter

Like Skye Warren on Facebook:
facebook.com/skyewarren

Join Skye Warren's Dark Room reader group:
skyewarren.com/darkroom

Follow Skye Warren on Instagram:
instagram.com/skyewarrenbooks

Visit Skye's website for her current booklist:
www.skyewarren.com/books

Acknowledgments

Thank you to Molly O'Keefe for being a story genius and for holding my hand when I need it. Thank you to Annika Martin and Rebecca at Fairest Reviews Editing for helping make the book better. Thank you to Ann and Ojhoana for your amazing insights, and to Dylan Allen for sending them to me. Thank you to Judy and Monique for your great catches.

And very special thanks to Annabel Joseph for Cirque du Monde, the show that Bethany and Romeo come from in CONCERTO. Cirque du Monde is Annabel's creation, originally found in her Cirque Masters series. I love Annabel's books so much and re-read them all the time.

Copyright

This is a work of fiction. Any resemblance to actual persons, living or dead, business establishments, events or locales is entirely coincidental. All rights reserved. Except for use in a review, the reproduction or use of this work in any part is forbidden without the express written permission of the author.

Concerto © 2019 by Skye Warren
Print Edition

Cover design by Book Beautiful
Formatted by BB eBooks

Made in the USA
Columbia, SC
26 August 2019